W.i.t.c.h.

Will Irma Taranee Cornelia Hay Lin

The Fire of Friendship

Adapted by ELIZABETH LENHARD

HarperCollins *Children's Books*

This book was first published in the USA in 2004 by Volo/Hyperion Books for Children
First published in Great Britain in 2005 by HarperCollins *Children's Books*, a division of
HarperCollins Publishers Ltd.

© 2005 Disney Enterprises, Inc.

ISBN 0-00-720938-X

1 3 5 7 9 10 8 6 4 2

The HarperCollins website is:
www.harpercollinschildrensbooks.co.uk

Visit www.clubwitch.co.uk

ONE

Hay Lin clutched the bus pole so hard her knuckles went white. She looked from Cornelia to Will and back to Cornelia again. Cornelia's thin lips were pulled so taut they matched Hay Lin's knuckles. And Will's face – pale with anger and worry – fit into the colour scheme, too.

Great, just great, Hay Lin thought. When we first learned that we had magical powers, I thought it was going to add some spice to our lives. Instead, it's drained us of all our colour!

And if Hay Lin needed *anything* in her life, it was colour – in the paint she splashed on her art projects, the Magic Markers she used to scrawl impromptu ideas on her palm, and the kooky outfits she devised every morning to wear. Today, for instance, Hay Lin was a vision of purple – purple leg warmers bunched around her ankles; lavender goggles cocked jauntily on top of her glossy, black hair; a swishy, eggplant miniskirt; and a bright fuchsia book bag.

And let's not forget the *other* colour in Hay Lin's life – the silvery swirls that burst from her palms every time she unleashed her magic. Hay Lin had power over the element of air – which meant she had an ability to make even the heaviest objects fly about like a dandelion seed on a breeze.

Her friends controlled elements, too. Cornelia's viny green, magical wisps manipulated the earth, from its soil to its leaves to its trees. Irma's shimmery blue powers were all about water. And Taranee's searing orange rays controlled fire.

As for Will, she was the keeper of the Heart of Candracar – a glass orb that shot rays of hot-pink light and transformed all five girls into superbeings. In those alternative forms, the friends were more knowing and more beautiful. They were decked out in the coolest clothes. They even had wings!

And why had Hay Lin and her four friends –

otherwise-ordinary schoolgirls at the Sheffield Institute – suddenly been infused with this magic? As Hay Lin's grandmother had explained to them right before she'd passed away, an Oracle in an ethereal place called Candracar had anointed them as Guardians of the Veil. The Veil was a barrier that this mystical, all-powerful being had placed between earth and the evil world of Metamoor. In Metamoor a snakelike villain, his lumpish, blue henchmen, and a mysterious and definitely evil prince named Phobos reigned.

At the end of every millennium, the Veil underwent a nasty change. It thinned and weakened, and even suffered some damage – tears in the supernatural fabric. Those tears had turned into a series of cosmic doorways: twelve portals. And those portals – all located somewhere in the Guardians' seaside city of Heatherfield – were direct routes to earth for the baddies of Metamoor.

That's where the Guardians came in. The Oracle had put them in charge of finding the portals and closing them with their newfound magic.

That alone is a megatask, Hay Lin thought.

But now, closing the portals isn't even at the top of our priority list! Instead, we have to focus on rescuing Taranee from Elyon.

It seemed only yesterday that Elyon had been one of them – a wispy, boy-crazy, sweet Sheffielder. But then she'd met a snaky Metamoorian who had been posing as a cute guy. The next thing the Guardians knew, Elyon had traveled through a portal to evil Metamoor and taken up residence there. Since then, she'd been doing everything she could to make sure the Guardians defected to the dark side. She'd even helped the Meridian army capture Taranee!

And that's why the remaining girls were bussing it to one of the portals to Metamoor – a magical window that had opened in the attic of Mrs. Rudolph's house.

And who is Mrs. Rudolph? Hay Lin thought drily. Oh, she's just a big, potbellied, scaly, dreadlocked, Metamoorian creature who has been masquerading as our *maths* teacher!

I mean, if anyone in our group is gonna get a kick out of creatures from another world, Hay Lin thought, it's me. I'm always up for a tall tale. But, c'mon! An algebra-teacher-turned-ogre?! That's outrageous. Of course, on another level, it makes perfect sense! I always thought maths was a monstrous subject.

Hay Lin tried to force a grin. She even thought of telling Irma her little joke. Irma – Hay Lin's constant partner in mischief – could always be counted on for a good giggle. *Except* at this particular moment, when Cornelia was sniping at Will and Will was sobbing on Hay Lin's shoulder – and they were all minutes away from going into Mrs. Rudolph's house, marching up to her attic, and traveling through the portal to rescue Taranee.

When the bus shuddered to a halt on Mrs. Rudolph's corner, the sulky, sniffly quartet got off in silence. They tromped towards Mrs. Rudolph's imposing pink house. As they walked, Hay Lin peeked at her friends. Will's tears had dried, and she was looking angrily determined. Cornelia was intense, as always, and Irma was wide-eyed.

But for some reason, Hay Lin was feeling fuzzy. Distracted. Not quite herself.

Maybe it's the bad vibes among my friends that's got me out of whack, she thought. Or maybe it's the fear. After all, I'm in no hurry to go back to Metamoor, where all the buildings are like dank, medieval castles, and all the inhabitants have bright blue skin or look like iguanas wearing tights and tunics.

She shuddered. Talk about creepy.

Whatever Hay Lin's yucky feeling was, it only intensified as Irma fished Mrs. Rudolph's house key out from under a planter on the front porch and unlocked the front door. It got stronger still as the girls padded up the elegant staircase to Mrs. Rudolph's top floor, then climbed the rickety stepladder into the attic.

When Will stood in front of the far wall of the attic – where the portal had opened before – and stretched out her magical hands, Hay Lin had to restrain herself from running in the opposite direction! Instead, she simply cringed.

Will closed her eyes and turned her palms upwards. From her right palm emerged a glowing spherical amulet – a clear, glass orb in an asymmetrical silver clasp. This was it. The Heart of Candracar – the unfathomable, mystical power that lived within Will's body.

The heart shimmered and pulsed with pink light. But . . . nothing happened! The wall remained just a wall. Hay Lin unclenched her skinny shoulders and stopped squinting. Then she watched in a daze as the girls glanced at each other worriedly.

"So?" Cornelia demanded sulkily.

Will sighed and lowered her hands.

"Nothing!" she said in surprise. "The portal won't open again."

She peered into the Heart of Candracar.

"The Seal of Phobos isn't giving any signs of life, either," she said with a frown.

The Seal of Phobos was a green-and-white, pointy-topped symbol of all that was bad in the world. Recently, the Seal had erupted in Cornelia's bedroom, threatening to trap all of the Guardians in suffocating, black gunk. The Heart of Candracar had saved them. In fact, it had kicked the Seal's butt, absorbing it right into its own crystal sphere.

The girls didn't know exactly what the Seal meant, but they did know that it played a role in opening the portals in the Veil. They were hoping it would lead them to Metamoor.

"I guess," Irma pointed out with a shrug, "the Seal helps us leave Metamoor. But entering it is another thing altogether!"

Will clasped her fist around the Heart.

"We can't leave Taranee!" she declared. "We'll find a portal that's still open, and we'll cross through there! Are you with me?"

She shot desperate looks at her companions. Cornelia nodded in sullen assent. Irma, on the other hand, was practically jumping with eagerness.

"No need to ask me!" she said. "I'm so there."

Then Irma turned to Hay Lin.

"Have you got the map of the portals?" she asked.

Hay Lin nodded slowly. Just the mention of the dusty, highly detailed map – which was slowly revealing the sites of Heatherfield's portals – made Hay Lin feel sad and heavy. After all, that map had been her grandmother's last gift to her before she had died. With it, she'd revealed to Hay Lin that she had once been a Guardian herself.

She had passed her legacy on to Hay Lin, and she had peacefully, happily returned to Candracar – leaving Hay Lin to fight this battle with only her friends for help.

Hay Lin suddenly felt limp with fatigue. In

fact, she felt . . . somehow . . . compelled to get out of the attic altogether! Hay Lin knew it was crucial that they find another portal on the magical map. After all, every minute they waited was another minute Taranee had to stay in some Metamoorian prison. But at that moment, none of that mattered. Hay Lin *had* to get out of there. So she reached into her book bag and pulled out the map. Its rough parchment felt dusty and dry in her hand. She gave the scroll to Will and said, "Here it is. But I'm leaving this one to you. I . . . I have to go."

As if in a trance, Hay Lin turned and crossed the wide attic floor. She was vaguely aware of her friends' curious stares boring into her back. Dimly, she heard Cornelia say, "What's up with her?"

"Dunno," Irma replied, "She's been acting a little weird ever since we got here."

The sound of Will's voice cut in. It was filled with awe.

"Look, you guys!" she cried. "The Heart of Candracar is showing us the way to the next portal. . . ."

Hay Lin knew that the Heart must have risen out of Will's hand and drifted to a spot on the Heatherfield map. Now that spot would be glowing bright pink – a sign that a portal could be found there.

Hay Lin also knew that she, too, should have been curious about the portal's location. She should have dashed back across the attic to check out the sitch. But *something* was drawing her down the steps, and she was powerless to resist it.

She drifted down the attic's ladder and headed toward the main stairwell.

With each step, Hay Lin felt lighter – more floaty. She was barely aware that she was walking at all. In fact, she wasn't!

My element is air, she thought, with her eyes closed. It's carrying me somewhere; telling me something. If Grandmother were here, I know just what she would say: "Be still, my little Hay Lin. Be still . . . and listen!"

So, when silvery magic began swooping around her, drawing her towards a little table in the front hall, Hay Lin didn't resist. She followed the silvery swirls. They began to flutter around an object on the table – a gold-painted, ceramic urn of some sort. It was round and squat, with an ornate, domed lid.

Hay Lin picked the urn up. She saw a tiny windup key sticking out of its side. The top of the urn was attached to the body with little hinges.

"I know what this is," Hay Lin murmured softly. "It's a music box."

Eyes wide with curiosity, she tipped the lid. She was right. A little song began to chime. It was as ethereal as an angel's voice. The tune was utterly foreign to Hay Lin, yet it was spellbinding.

Even more fascinating than the music was the tiny, porcelain figure inside the box. It was a young girl in a ballerina's dress. She had feathery wings that looked remarkably like the Guardians', and a benevolent expression etched on her tiny face. Her arms were outstretched, and one leg was pointed behind her. She was a fairy, poised for flight.

How odd, Hay Lin thought dreamily as she watched the little figure twirl to the lilting music. I've never heard this song before, but it reminds me of something. . . .

Suddenly, images flooded into Hay Lin's head: Ghostly beings. Frantic movement. Flight.

Hay Lin closed her eyes, and the picture grew clearer. In a wash of silver light, she made out two figures, both cloaked in hooded, brown robes.

One looked like . . . Mrs. Rudolph! The Metamoorian Mrs. Rudolph anyway, with her ropy dreadlocks, red horns dotting her thick neck, floppy ears, and squashy snout.

The other person looked more like a human female. She was thin and wiry, the skin on her face pulled taut with anguish. Her hair erupted from beneath her hood, flying around her head in frantic tendrils. She looked terrified.

Perhaps . . . Hay Lin thought hazily, she's scared of losing that bundle she holds so tightly. She's cradling it as if it's something sacred. It's . . . it's . . .

Hay Lin frowned as the fuzzy image of the bundle became clearer.

It's . . . Hay Lin realised suddenly – it's a baby!

The baby was beautiful. She had fair skin and pouty lips. Her wide-set, pale-blue eyes seemed to look out at the world with a sad sense of some deeper knowledge.

In fact, the baby seemed even to regard

Hay Lin – who was gazing down into this daydream – with calm recognition. And the eerie thing was, Hay Lin felt that she knew the infant, too! The familiarity hit her with a jolt.

In fact, it threw her off balance! As she stumbled forward, her eyes popped open, and the music box flew from her hands.

"Oh!" she squealed, as the pretty box fell to the floor with a crash. It broke into a dozen pieces. The golden dancer's arm broke off at the elbow. But its sweet, smiling face remained intact.

Hay Lin stared at the little figure for a moment. The pounding of her friends' feet on the stairs jolted her from her reverie.

"Hay Lin!" Will cried. "Is everything all right?"

As Hay Lin looked up at her friends, the fog in her head quickly dissipated. Her thoughts began rushing in faster and clearer now.

"I . . . I think it is! The song that came out of that music box . . . " Hay Lin began, pointing at the shards at her feet. "It made me remember something!"

"So?" Irma said gently. "A lot of songs remind us of things that have happened to us."

"Yeah, but this song – I'd never heard it before," Hay Lin cried. "The memory – it wasn't mine! I saw these creatures crossing through the portal in the attic. I could feel their fear! And I saw the face of a little girl – a face I would know anywhere!"

"Hay Lin," Will said, grabbing Hay Lin's hand. "Maybe you've just discovered a new power!" .

"Do you mean to say," Cornelia asked, planting her hands on her hips skeptically, "that she sees the memories of others by listening to their favourite music?"

"Right," Will said. "And that music box there belonged to Mrs. Rudolph!"

"Exactly," Irma said, stepping forward and nudging a piece of the box with her sneakered toe. "Mrs. Rudolph comes from Metamoor. Obviously, Hay Lin saw what happened the day she arrived here in Heatherfield."

Hay Lin sighed, feeling a big weight lift from her shoulders. She had a new power! And what's more, her friends understood her new power. They didn't balk in disbelief. They didn't fight against the magic, just because it was foreign and weird. After all they'd been through –

from having conversations with Will's talking appliances to visiting Metamoor – they were taking this latest development in stride.

This can only help us in our fight against the Metamoorians, Hay Lin thought gleefully.

A moment later, she turned the phrase over in her head again: *our fight against the Metamoorians.* Then her joy evaporated as quickly as it had materialised.

If I've learned anything, Hay Lin thought wearily, it's that no security lasts for long when you're a Guardian of the Veil.

She looked at her friends with somber eyes.

"If what you're saying is true," she said to Irma, "that I've just recalled Mrs. Rudolph's arrival here on earth, then I wonder – why was she so scared? And what was she escaping from? Because whatever it is, we're bound to face it, too!"

TWO

With her fellow Guardians, Irma slipped out of Mrs. Rudolph's house and tiptoed across the porch. She glanced around apprehensively as she slipped the key back under its planter.

We can't let anyone see that we've basically broken into Mrs. Rudolph's house, she thought breathlessly. I can just see the headline in tomorrow morning's paper: "Police Sergeant's Daughter Arrested for Breaking and Entering."

Forget about saving the world after that, Irma thought with a shudder. I'd be so grounded, I'd forget what the world *looks* like.

As soon as the girls had gone down the walk and through Mrs. Rudolph's gate, Irma sighed with relief. A moment later, she felt a familiar sense of pleasure come over her. She giggled softly. *Nothing* beat the rush of getting away with something!

With a burst of energy, she turned to Hay Lin, Cornelia, and Will.

"Are we still meeting at the shell cave at eight?" Irma asked.

"The shell cave?" Hay Lin asked, with wide eyes. "That big old cavern where we used to hide when we were kids? Why are we going there?"

"Oh, right," Will said. "You were downstairs when the Heart of Candracar showed us the site of the next portal – it's in the shell cave."

"Cool," Hay Lin said. She took the portal map back from Will and stuffed it into her book bag. "It'll be nice to go somewhere where we don't have to pick a lock! All this breaking and entering makes me nervous."

"*Tscha!*" Irma said with a vigorous nod. "Let's head home and change into more suit-able gear. We'll meet up in a little bit."

Irma turned to Will and Cornelia. They both lived in the opposite direction from Irma's and Hay Lin's homes.

"See you soon!" Irma said, smiling and

waving goodbye to them.

"Yup," Cornelia said grimly. "Don't be late, Irma."

"Am I ever?" Irma asked challengingly.

"Um, only all the time," Cornelia retorted.

Irma was just about to get good and mad when she felt Hay Lin's little hand on her shoulder.

"No fighting," she declared. "And besides, Cornelia's right, Irma. You *are* always late."

Irma frowned for a moment and then shrugged.

"You're right," she said with a grin. "I admit it. But this time, I won't be. I promise. We're doing this for Taranee. I won't let her down!"

Will shot Irma a grateful smile, and then the girls parted. As Hay Lin and Irma tromped through the cool, autumn breeze towards Irma's butter-yellow house, Hay Lin glanced at her.

"Where did you tell your parents you were," she asked, "while we were at Mrs. Rudolph's?"

"At your place, of course," Irma responded with a grin. "I told them we were eating at your parents' Chinese restaurant. So make sure you cover for me if you have to."

Hay Lin nodded with a grin. But as the girls stopped at the bottom of Irma's driveway, Irma crossed her hands over her stomach and frowned.

"There's only one problem with my master scheme," she said. "We *didn't* actually eat dinner, and I'm still hungry. I'm going to have to raid the fridge before I head out."

"Good plan," Hay Lin said, turning to continue down the street towards the Silver Dragon. She lived with her parents in a cosy apartment above the family restaurant. "See you later, *you know where!*"

"Count on it," Irma said as she fished her house keys out of her book bag. Then she tiptoed up the path behind her house. All she had to do was slip silently through the kitchen door, grab some grub, and dash upstairs to change.

I really hope nobody's around, she thought as she gently turned her key in the lock and eased open the kitchen door. The last thing I want to do is answer any awkward questions, such as . . .

"Where have you been!?"

Yeah, such as that! Irma thought with a

grimace. Then she peeked guiltily around the door. Yup! There was her mum, blocking her path, a clenched fist on each hip.

Irma felt her cheeks go hot. But she tried to give her mum one of her usual, cocky grins.

"I've been . . ." she began.

"I called Hay Lin's restaurant," Mum cut in with an arched eyebrow. "They told me you weren't there."

"Of course not, Mum," Irma said with a shrug. "Because . . . we got the food to go! Then we went over to Will's to eat."

Good save! Irma told herself with a smile. Triumphantly, she shrugged herself out of her jacket and headed for the stairs. She'd change first and cop some chow from the kitchen when the coast was clear. She was halfway up the steps, with visions of her favourite pink sweatshirt in her head, when her mother's voice stopped her cold.

"Don't run off, Miss Always-Ready-With-An-Answer," Mum called to her, from the foyer at the base of the stairs. Irma felt the hairs stand up on the back of her neck.

So close to escape, she thought in anguish, yet so far! What did I do wrong? Maybe Mum called Will's house, too? So she knows we weren't there like I told her!

Irma's creative juices were frantically churning to come up with a new story, when she saw her mother . . . *smile* at her. And then something even more miraculous happened.

"There's a surprise for you in the living room," Mum announced.

"Really?!" Irma shrieked. "I mean, uh," she said more quietly, "really?" She ran a calming hand over her tousled brown hair and admonished herself: Cool it. Act too relieved, and Mum will *know* something's up.

So, with faux casualness, Irma added, "Is this surprise, say, something to eat?"

That's when Christopher poked his head into the foyer. As usual, Irma gazed at her unkempt little brother. He responded with a gap-toothed grin and a taunting hint: "Naw, this guy is too big to eat!"

Then, with a wicked and mischievous cackle, Christopher turned on his heel and ran back into the living room.

Irma's feet remained rooted to her spot on the steps – probably because, at the mention of a certain word, her legs had lapsed into a state of sudden and absolute paralysis.

Guy.

Guy?!?

Irma began frantically smoothing down her wind-ruffled hair as she tried to imagine what guy could possibly be camped out in her living room. The living room of her very house.

Was it Ulysses Sherman – the boy she'd been crushing on ever since he'd waltzed into her biology class earlier in the year? Or maybe it was Joshua Anderson. Irma *thought* she'd seen him shoot her a flirty look in the cafeteria yesterday. Okay, maybe he'd just been eyeing the chocolate cupcakes on Irma's lunch tray, but . . .

Suddenly Irma gasped.

Maybe it was Hank Dubrovnik – the quarterback of the Sheffield football team! He was two years older than Irma. He had shiny, black hair and sparkly, green eyes and a chin dusted with stubble. He also had no idea Irma was alive.

But what the heck, Irma thought with a hopeful shrug. If I can have magical powers, anything's possible, right?

Irma pasted her most flirtatious smile onto

her lips, smoothed her pink sweater over her hips, and headed for the living-room door.

"Hi . . ." she said, catching sight of the boy on the couch. But that was the last word she was able to choke out.

Guy?! That showed how much Christopher knew! This was no guy! This was . . . Martin Tubbs! Skinny, geeky, and oh-so-annoying Martin Tubbs. He was everywhere Irma turned, waggling his shaggy blond eyebrows at her. Asking her out on a date. Or just salivating in her presence. Awful, awful–

"Martin!" Irma snarled with a curled lip.

"Oh, yeah," Christopher piped up. He was sitting on a chair next to the couch, grinning at a spiral-bound notebook in his lap. "That was his name."

Irma ignored her pesky brother and stormed over to the couch. Martin jumped to his feet and gave her one of his trademark, goofy grins. Then he proudly tweaked a blue kerchief tied around his neck.

"How did you get in here?" Irma demanded. "And why are you dressed like that?"

In addition to his strange neck gear, Martin was wearing an army-green shirt with shiny brass buttons and epaulets. He also wore green cargo shorts, blue, woolly socks, and hiking boots.

Martin nodded at Irma's father, who was standing behind the couch, straightening his tie as he got ready for the night shift.

"Hi, honey," Dad said to Irma with a wave. "Nice young man, this Martin."

"Thanks, Sergeant Lair," Martin piped up. Then he planted his swooning gaze back upon Irma.

"In answer to your questions," he said, "your father let me in. And I'm dressed like this because I'm an Explorer Scout. Our troop is called the Happy Bears. In fact, I brought you a Happy Bears calendar!"

Martin pointed to the green notebook in Christopher's grimy little paws.

"Normally, we charge for those calendars," he said, turning back to Irma with a gooey smile. "But for you – it's a present."

Oh. My. God, Irma thought queasily. This moment could not get any more disgusting.

"Hey, look!" Christopher declared from behind Martin. He was grinning at one of the calendar pages. "This month, there's a picture of two lovebirds in here!"

Oh. My. God, Irma thought again. I was wrong!

She ignored her brother and continued to glare at Martin.

"Spit it out, Martin," she said. "If you don't want money for that calendar, what *do* you want?"

"Well . . ." Martin said, clasping his hands hopefully. "Now that you mention it, some of the other Bears and I are getting together tonight to look at slides from our last camping trip. Would you . . . care to join us?"

Irma could feel a tingling in her fingertips. She recognised that feeling. It was her magic, bristling to get out. It wanted to whip up a quick little tidal wave to wash Martin from the room. Or maybe a black cloud that would follow him all the way home? Or . . .

Suddenly, Irma shook her head and pressed her tingling fingers into her palms.

Don't do this again, she warned herself.

After all, Irma's magic had gotten her into trouble before. At the Sheffield Halloween party, for instance, when she'd told Martin to disappear, he actually *had*. The guy had become invisible for a full hour.

Then, when a boy named Andrew Hornby had gotten a little too touchy-feely with Irma on a date, she'd turned him into a toad! She and the other Guardians had had to spend an entire afternoon in the Heatherfield nature preserve searching for the warty little varmint so that they could turn him back into a person.

A toad named Martin was sounding pretty good to Irma right about now. But she didn't have time to deal with the fallout. Not when Taranee and the other Guardians were counting on her.

So with her fists still clenched and her jaw practically grinding with the effort, Irma smiled at Martin. Then she said, softly, and as nicely as possible, "No, thank you!"

"But – but, it will be a lot of fun," Martin protested.

"Uh-huh," Irma said. She grabbed Martin's shoulders and spun him around. She started shoving him towards the front door.

"We've got a musical group, too!" Martin said desperately.

"Oh, I think I've heard of them," Irma cracked rudely as she gave Martin one last shove that sent him tripping out onto the front porch. "The Bear Growls, right?"

Martin opened his mouth to respond, but before he could utter a word, Irma slammed the door in his face.

She spun around and leaned back against the door, huffing with frustration. It didn't help that her parents were standing in the hallway, regarding her with giggly smiles.

"I don't know why you don't like him," Dad said, pulling on his police officer's coat. "A man in uniform is pretty dashing. At least, your mother seems to think so!"

Mum handed Dad his officer's cap with a smirk.

"Maybe a few sizes ago," she teased as she playfully eyed his round belly.

"Ha-ha-ha!" Irma chortled. Then, out of the corner of her eye, she saw Christopher sidle out of the living room.

"And you!" she barked, running towards him. "'This month there's a picture of two love-birds'!? What were you *thinking*?"

"I was thinking that . . . the bathroom would make an excellent getaway!" Christopher squealed. He pounded across the foyer and threw himself into the downstairs bathroom, slamming the door and locking it.

"Ha-ha, big sister," he taunted from behind the door. "Catch me now, if you can!"

"If you say so," Irma whispered, with a scheming smile. She planted both palms on the bathroom door. Then she shut her eyes and felt her magic begin to bubble up within her. A swirl of blue energy pulsed from her palms. Irma could imagine the whirling, watery magic making its way through the bathroom door, then wafting over to, say, the shower.

No sooner had Irma conjured up the image than Christopher started shrieking.

"Aaaagh!" he cried. "Mummy! Daddy!"

Irma's parents thundered over to the bathroom door. Irma sidestepped them neatly and made her way to the stairs.

"What's happening in there?" Dad roared, as Mum jiggled the doorknob in alarm.

"Water is pouring out of the shower!" Christopher's voice squeaked. "And I'm getting all wet!"

Irma smiled with satisfaction and blew a wispy remnant of magic from her index finger. Magical powers made taking care of pesky little brothers a whole lot easier. Now if only she could solve the issue of Metamoor's baddies as easily.

"*I'm* getting out of here," she muttered to herself. "The portal to Metamoor is waiting! We've got some kidnappers to deal with!"

THREE

Will stood in her bedroom, checking off items on a mental list.

Sneakers with good soles for running from Metamoorian bad guys? she thought, with a glance at her feet. Check.

A warm raincoat for weathering rain, snow, or even a tornado? (After all, who knew what season it was in Metamoor, much less what the weather awaiting them would be?) Check.

Granola bars and a brimming water bottle? Check.

"I guess I'm all set, then," Will said, looking around her room. Her eyes fell on her unmade bed, and she cringed guiltily. The least she could do before she left her mum – perhaps forever – was to tidy up her bedroom.

Will glanced at her watch. She had to meet her friends at the shell cave soon. There just wasn't time.

And besides, Will thought, indignantly, why should I do my mum any favours when I'm totally mad at her?

And why was Will mad? Because she'd recently spotted her mother holding hands with a man. In public! Since Will's parents were divorced, this sort of behavior was *technically* okay. But the fact that the man had been Will's history teacher was definitely *not* okay. In fact, it was downright humiliating! If Mum wants to go off and start dating Mr. Collins without even telling me, Will thought, well, I can very well leave my bed unmade while I go off to an alternate universe.

"So, there," she added out loud, giving her disheveled bedclothes a defiant glare.

"*Rrrrr,*" the bed responded. Then the comforter began bouncing up and down.

"Aaaagh!" Will squealed. "First, the fridge and all my other electrical appliances start talking to me. Now my furniture is talking, too?!"

"*Rrrrr,*" the bed said again. A whiskery, brown face poked out from beneath the comforter and wiggled its nose at Will.

"Silly dormouse!" Will cried, pouncing on the bed and scooping up her pet dormouse. "I almost forgot about you."

She scratched the brown, squirrel-like critter's little, round ears and gave it a kiss goodbye. But before she let it scurry away again, she stopped to think.

"Wait a minute," she whispered. "What if I really don't come back from Meridian? Or I do come back, but it takes me a really long time? What'll happen to you, little guy?"

Will thought back to the day she'd rescued her dormouse from Uriah, Sheffield's leading bully. Uriah had been trying to capture the dormouse and put it into goofy Martin Tubbs's locker.

Will had chased Uriah and his lugheaded gang out of Heatherfield Park. And that's when Matt Olsen had ambled along.

At first, Will had expected Matt to be like every other guy she'd met in this town.

But he'd been about as different from the rest as anybody could get. Matt had bundled up the dormouse in his sweater, told Will all about the care and feeding of the fluffy-tailed critters, and even given her his number, in case she had any questions for him.

Of course, Will thought dreamily, he was probably thinking I'd have *dormouse* questions, when what I really wanted to ask him was, how did you get so cute? What are you doing Friday night? How could a hip lead singer in a band possibly be so sweet?! And, of course, the big question – when can I see you again?

Will hadn't, of course, asked Matt any of those questions that day. In fact, she'd barely had the nerve to squeak, "Goodbye."

Will's shoulders slumped as she pondered her unrequited crush. And the long journey to Meridian ahead of her. *And* the plight of her little, soon-to-be-orphaned (well, maybe!) dormouse.

Then she figured out just what to do!

She picked up the dormouse and stuffed it into its favourite hiding place – her backpack. Then she grabbed her bicycle and darted out of the apartment.

As she pedaled through the waning light of the day, a little voice in the back of Will's head chastised her.

Oh, you're so concerned for your dormouse,

eh? it said. *You're not just using this little animal as an excuse to see cute, brown-eyed Matt Olsen, are you?*

"No!" Will muttered to herself. "Please – I'm just asking Matt for a favour. Any responsible pet owner would. And, well, if he wants to give me a smooch, too . . ."

The thought of locking lips with Matt made Will flush bright red. As she coasted down the hill towards her crush's house, she shook her head. Stop dreaming, she told herself. Even if I am going off to another world, perhaps never to see Matt again, there's no way I would have the courage to kiss him. I could never do that – he's way too cute!

With the image of that dream kiss lingering in her head, Will didn't think she could ever face Matt at all!

He's probably not home, anyway, she thought, as she skidded to a stop in front of his house. I'll just leave the dormouse in his front yard and tie a little note around its neck.

Dismounting from her bike, Will looked up at Matt's house. It was a cute Victorian house with a big cupola that angled off the roof.

I wonder if that's Matt's room, Will thought

dreamily. The front yard was a bit scruffy and overgrown. Darting around inside the slightly dilapidated fence were a few cats, a puppy, and even a squawking parrot!

Well, this *must* be the right place, she thought. Only the grandson of a veterinarian would have this many critters running around. I hope Matt doesn't mind having one more on his hands for a while.

Will slipped her backpack off her shoulders and pulled out the dormouse. The little animal looked up at the parrot – which had fluttered up to perch on one of the fence posts – and unleashed a series of nervous little peeps.

"Relax," Will whispered, stroking the little guy's head tenderly. With her other hand, she rifled around in her backpack for a scrap of paper and a pen. But the dormouse was squirming in her arms so much now that she couldn't hang on to it.

Oh, forget it, Will thought, letting the animal hop out of her arms and scamper into Matt's yard. She followed it through the front gate and hesitated. There was no way a note was going to stay attached to her hyperactive little dormouse as it explored its temporary home.

I know, Will thought, reaching into her backpack again. I'll send Matt an e-mail from my cell phone.

As the dormouse scampered through the long grass, Will dashed off a quick note to Matt's e-mail address:

Dear Matt, she wrote, smiling to herself as she typed in the cutie's name. *Something's come up and I'm not going to be able to take care of my dormouse for a few days. Would you mind keeping an eye on him? You're the only one I could trust. Thanks a bunch! Will.*

With another wistful smile, Will hit SEND.

Then she giggled and typed in a P.S. *Oh, and could you take care of me, too?* she wrote. She laughed again and deleted the wishful P.S.

"I won't send that one," she whispered to herself. Then she jumped. What was that?

Creaaaaak!

Matt's front door was opening. As the crack in the doorway widened, Will saw both the toe of a big, floppy sneaker and a blue sweatshirt edging their way outside. It had to be Matt!

Glancing desperately around the yard, Will saw a shrub – actually more like a tangle of vines and leaves – near the fence. She scrambled behind the short bush and fell to the ground, hugging her knees and squeezing her eyes shut.

Why didn't I think he'd be home? She thought, berating herself. I hope he didn't see me!

Fearfully, she opened one eye and peeked through the leaves at Matt. He was gazing around the yard with a good-natured smile. Then the dormouse scampered up to his toe.

"Ah, there you are, dormouse," he said. Then he looked around the yard. "But where's your friend?"

Oh, man! Will thought, biting her lip. I'll definitely send a note next time. E-mails arrive way too fast!

When Matt didn't see her, he shrugged and grabbed the brown fuzzy animal up into his arms. He tickled the little guy under its chin and ran his hand over its fur. Will felt a little jealous.

Oh, if only I were a dormouse, she mused.

She raised herself out of the bush to get a better view. Then she heaved a big sigh.

Too big a sigh.

Matt twisted around to look her way. Will

stifled a yelp and ducked back into the shrubs, reaching for a couple of vines to stop herself from falling.

"Did you hear something?" Matt asked the little dormouse. He peered at the shrub and scratched the animal's ears absentmindedly. Will cringed and waited to see if she'd been caught. Apparently, she hadn't.

Matt merely shrugged and turned to head back into his house. The dormouse scampered up the boy's shoulder as he walked toward the door.

Will sighed with relief – until, that is, Matt made one last casual comment to the dormouse before stepping inside.

"I've really got to do some weeding in that shrubbery," he said. "Who knows what kind of bugs are lurking in that nettle bush?"

With that, the door slammed shut, whereupon Will looked around her in alarm.

Bugs?! she thought. Did he say bugs? I *hate* bugs.

Pulling on the vines more tightly, she got to her feet and darted out from behind the shrub. She hopped around and brushed off her clothes. When she'd judged herself to be bug-free, she sighed with relief.

But, as Will hurried back to her bike, she became aware of something else. Though there were no insects crawling around beneath her clothes, she was still feeling decidedly itchy.

That was when she remembered Matt's *entire* sentence: *Who knows what kind of bugs are lurking in that* nettle *bush!*

Nettles! Will thought in dismay. She looked at her palms. And her wrists. And her ankles. Sure enough, hot, pink, and very itchy welts were beginning to rise up on every bit of skin that had touched the shrubbery.

Just great, Will thought, jumping onto her bike. She looked at her watch, then gave herself one good scratch before she started pedaling madly for the shell cave.

I'm going to be late to meet the other Guardians, *and* I'm an itch-monster, Will thought with a sigh. If I didn't know better, I'd say having a crush was as dangerous as battling creatures from Metamoor!

FOUR

Cornelia stood at the edge of the water. She crossed her long arms over her chest and gazed out over the water. The stretch of buildings that made up Heatherfield was just beginning to glitter with evening lights. Cornelia thought she could even make out the steel-and-glass sky-scraper where she lived.

Beyond that tableau, the sky was turning flame-orange as the sun set. It looked shimmery and almost painfully pretty. As it dipped ever lower in the horizon, Cornelia shook her head over the contradiction of it all. There was the sun – a serene, beautiful, perfect sphere, getting ready to dunk itself into the roiling, cold ocean.

I know just how the sun must feel,

Cornelia thought with a sigh. I was living this life that anybody would call charmed. I have a fabulous wardrobe. Skating medals. A nice-enough family, if you don't count my annoying little sister, Lilian. And most of all, an amazing group of friends. Friends I could always count on to be there for me.

Now, my nice, orderly life is about to be plunged into chaos.

That stinks, she continued to muse petulantly. Especially since the girl who got us into our latest round of chaos can't even be bothered to show up on time! I mean, first *she* makes an executive decision to leave Taranee in Metamoor. Then she disses us. Some leader!

"Where is Will? It's cold here," Cornelia said brusquely, turning to look at Irma and Hay Lin. They had arrived just after she had. Now they were standing behind her, huddling for warmth in their coats and rubbing their hands in the wind.

"She called me to say she's running a little late," Irma said with a shrug. "I think she wanted to take a shower."

As Irma spoke, a particularly large breaker crashed onto the sand. Cornelia had to skitter backward to avoid getting her sneakers soaked.

"We'll be taking a shower ourselves if we stay here much longer," she declared. "These waves are out of control!"

Irma flashed Cornelia one of her trademark, cocky grins – the kind that usually made Cornelia's blood boil. But this time, Irma had a welcome retort.

"Don't be afraid of the water, Cornelia," she said. "At least, not when I'm standing next to you!"

Irma planted her red shoes in the sand and turned to face another frothy wave that was headed straight for them. She threw her arms into the air. A shower of blue magic arced out into the ocean, dappling the giant wave just as it began to peak. The moment Irma's mystical blue stream hit the water, the wave seemed to stop in its tracks. In fact, it reared back like a shying horse! It flipped over, flinging itself back into the sea without ever connecting to the shore.

Irma turned to Cornelia and Hay Lin with a pleased smile and dusted sparks of excess magic off her hands. Cornelia felt a little spasm of jealousy. She knew how Irma was feeling just then. After all, Cornelia had used her own swirls of green magic to make vines grow instantly out of the earth. She'd bored through walls of thick brick and even metal. She'd sped up time and tidied her bedroom without lifting a finger. She'd known true power – and she'd been thrilled by it. But, unlike Irma, Cornelia felt compelled to rein her magic in when she was in public.

Our magic is a gift and a curse, she thought broodingly. *I'd never use it as frivolously as Irma does. Besides, what if someone saw us? They'd think we were circus freaks! We'd become instant Outfielders.*

Outfielders, of course, was the name given to the unpopular kids at Sheffield Institute. Cornelia had always been an Infielder at school and she *really* wanted to keep it that way. That meant keeping her magic a thoroughly private matter.

If that's even possible, Cornelia thought grimly. *Frankly, I feel like I'm losing control of this whole situation. I mean, Will's calling the shots. And, if I want to be a team player, I just have to go along with what she says.*

Cornelia was even more disturbed by the

mystery that surrounded Meridian. The place was only a dark and shadowy puzzle in her mind. She had no idea of what to expect when the girls crossed through the portal in a few minutes. She didn't even know if they'd survive this!

Of course, Irma and Hay Lin aren't thinking so bleakly, Cornelia thought, glancing at her grinning friends. They're still giddy over Irma's little parlour trick.

"I can't believe what you just did!" Hay Lin was sputtering to Irma. "Can you control all these waves?"

"Well," Irma said with false modesty. "It's not like I can make them go away. But I *can* ask them to take their foamy selves elsewhere!"

"Tell them to stay far away from our cave!" called a voice behind the three Guardians. They spun around in time to see Will pedaling her bike to the edge of the beach and grinding to a halt. She looked windblown and harassed. "I think it's time for us to head for that portal."

"Will," Irma breathed. "Finally!"

Giving them an apologetic look, Will got off her bike. Then the girls walked over to a huge, looming cave whose mouth was the shape of a perfect scallop shell. As they went inside, Irma said, "Since you've just arrived in town, Will, let me introduce you to the shell cave!"

"Kinda strange!" Will said, gazing up at the almost perfectly round, craggy ceiling. As she peered into the cave's gloom, she scratched her neck. Then she scratched one of her wrists. Then she moved back to her neck, *scritch-scritch-scritch*ing away.

"What's up?" Hay Lin asked, giving Will a fishy look. "Why are you scratching yourself?"

"Because nettle bushes have hateful, irritating leaves!" Will said with a grimace – and another scratch.

"That's not really an answer, is it?" Hay Lin replied with a cocked eyebrow and a sly grin.

"Well, it's the truth," Will said, becoming a bit pink in the cheeks. She didn't want to give her friends any specific details about her sudden itchiness.

"Okay, whatever," Cornelia said, butting in. "We've got some work to do. I think we should create some astral drops to substitute for us."

Hay Lin's face fell.

"Is that really necessary?" she squeaked.

"I don't know when we'll be coming back,"

Cornelia said with a curt nod. "To tell you the truth, I don't know *if* we'll come– "

"Of course, we'll come back, Cornelia," Will interrupted. "With Taranee!"

Cornelia turned to gaze at Will. "If you're so certain of that," she said, "then why don't you put your money where your mouth is? Make an astral drop with the rest of us, so we can be on our way to Metamoor."

She knew her voice was dripping with challenge. But that was just the way it had to be. If Will was going to fight her at every turn, she'd fight back!

"Be quiet, and I *will* whip up a double!" Will declared, sticking her chin out. "But I'm doing it for Taranee. Only for her!"

Will clamped her eyes shut and balled her hands into fists. Following her lead, Irma and Hay Lin became still, too. In fact, as they fell into states of deep concentration, they began to . . . glow! Streams of cool, blue light began to swirl around their bodies. The glow grew so bright and strong it began to stream out of the shell cave's entrance.

Cornelia closed her eyes as well. She imagined her astral drop – her double, her clone – separating from her. She envisioned that phantom Cornelia sleeping in her bed, kissing her sister good-night, flirting with boys in the halls at school. She felt a stab of pain at the idea of this specter – an intruder – living her life.

But then, Cornelia thought of Taranee – her friend, trapped in Metamoor. That made for a much sharper pang of grief.

It's worth it, Cornelia thought to herself, to help Taranee. After all, what is friendship, if not giving up a bit of yourself?

As the thought skimmed through Cornelia's mind, she felt suddenly lighter. She felt empty. She felt – a presence, hovering right in front of her face.

So Cornelia opened her eyes. She gave a yelp of surprise. A second Cornelia – three-dimensional and blinking in surprise – stood before her!

FIVE

Through her lowered eyelids, Will was dimly aware of a bright blue glow. It was swirling and shimmering around her and her fellow Guardians.

Abruptly, the light disappeared. Will felt the darkness return, like a light, cool cloak. In fact, she felt light from within, too! She had become somehow airy and ethereal and . . .

Suddenly, Will's mouth went dry.

I bet I know why I feel so light, she thought with a tremble. I think there's a bit of me that's missing – namely, my astral drop!

Sure enough, when Will's eyes popped open, she saw a version of herself standing right in front of her! The sight of her double was extremely disconcerting.

Are my knees really that knobby? she thought. *And, whoa, is that what the back of my head looks like?*

Will tried to shake off her freak-out.

Get a grip, she told herself. *It's not as if this is the first time you've doubled yourself. We all created astral drops in Metamoor once before, to provide decoys for those Metamoorian henchmen.*

But that had been a crisis situation. The moment the Guardians had spun out their astral drops, they'd sent the Metamoorians running after the doubles. Sure enough, Frost the Hunter had caught their astral drops – giving the *real* Guardians a chance to make a run for it. And they'd all gotten away – except Taranee.

The point was, Will hadn't had but a moment to contemplate her astral drop. Now, she was staring right at . . . her? It? What was she, or it, anyway, this other Will?

I know one thing that she, or it, is, Will thought as she watched her double begin exploring the shell cave. *She's a little loopy!*

Astral Will was spinning around in giddy circles, staring up at the ceiling with an empty little smile and twirling tendrils of her red hair around her fingertips absentmindedly.

Weird, Will thought. Then she shrugged. Well, I guess that's astral-drop behaviour, right? she mused.

She glanced at the other girls' doubles. She watched them walk like Cornelia, Irma, and Hay Lin. Talk like Cornelia, Irma, and Hay Lin. Even their eyes had the same ways of glimmering as Cornelia's, Irma's, and Hay Lin's. Will's shoulders climbed up to her ears nervously. She bit her lip as she watched her friends meet their astral selves.

"Amazing," Irma cried, as she stared at Astral Irma. "You are . . . me?"

As if she couldn't quite believe it were true, Irma reached out and tweaked Astral Irma's nose.

Astral Irma glared at the real Irma irritably and pulled away. "Hey!" she sniped. "Pinch your own nose!"

At that, Irma grinned. She turned to her friends (and their doubles) and declared, "I don't know about you, but I think I look *pret*-ty good!"

"All I know," Hay Lin said, staring at her

own astral drop in bewilderment, "is that I'm definitely seeing double."

"It's fantastic," Cornelia declared. Her astral drop was looking at her with a typically knowing smirk. "It's like looking at our reflections in a mirror!"

"Ooh, I hope not," Astral Cornelia retorted drily. She pointed at the actual Cornelia. "I'd like to think I'm prettier than *that!*"

Cornelia blinked at her double in utter amazement.

"What did you just say?!" she shrieked at, um, herself.

Irma rolled her eyes and smirked at Will.

"Oh, yes," she said with a glib nod. "They really are just like us."

"Uh," Will quavered. She was watching Astral Will slump onto a boulder at the shell cave's mouth. Her double looked positively lost. "Maybe not all of them!"

Suddenly, the other girls – even Cornelia and Astral Cornelia – fell silent. They all formed a circle around Astral Will. She responded with a blank, vacant stare.

"Er . . . *Will*," Irma said to Astral Will, with exaggerated slowness. "Where do you live?"

"I live in . . . um," Astral Will stuttered, "I live on a street in, um, a . . . place. . . ."

Will felt her heart sink as Irma threw up her hands.

"She's a blank!" Irma cried. "Empty! Zero!"

"I wonder how that happened," Hay Lin said to Will. "Our astral drops know everything we know – every sensation, every memory. And yours is just the opposite."

Will's mouth dropped open in dismay. Quickly, however, her shock turned to guilt. All at once, Will knew *exactly* how this had happened. It was all her fault!

She hung her head and stumbled away from her friends. In a small, trembly voice, she admitted, "While I was creating her, in the back of my mind, I was afraid that she would– "

"Take your place indefinitely?" Cornelia cut in. For the first time since the girls had arrived at the cave, Cornelia's harsh voice softened. Will looked up and caught her friend's gaze. Behind the hardness in Cornelia's eyes Will saw a glimmer of understanding.

Will and Cornelia had definitely had their differences since the memorable debacle in Metamoor, but at this moment, Will felt as though Cornelia were her best friend. Cornelia seemed to understand Will's fear that her astral drop might be just as special as – or perhaps even *more* special than – Will herself.

Will felt a surge of warmth and gratitude.

Of course, a moment later, a glance at Astral Will brought in a quick cold front. Sympathy from Cornelia wasn't going to make Will's problem go away.

And Irma's idea didn't seem feasible, either.

"Hey, if it's no good," she declared, "just make another one!"

"No," Cornelia said, shaking her head. "There's no guarantee that this won't happen all over again."

Will shook her head and sighed.

"Cornelia's right," she said to the group. "This is my problem, so I'll fix it. It should be easy enough!"

Will took her backpack off her shoulders and fished out a paper and pencil. She began making a list. A list of everything – *absolutely everything* – she did during the day, from brushing her teeth in the morning to stopping by her locker after lunch to watching *Boy Comet* on TV every Tuesday night.

After some careful and detailed jotting, Will thought she'd covered it all. She thrust the list into her double's hands. Astral Will read the list (at least she could read!), then gave Will a simple smile.

"Do you get this?" Will asked her severely. "On this paper, I've written everything you should and should *not* do. You can understand that, can't you, Will?"

Astral Will shrugged in a way that looked – Will had to admit it – pretty Will-like. Then she nodded and smiled sweetly.

Will felt her shoulders untense a bit.

Maybe this will work, she thought hopefully. All the astral me has to do is follow these simple instructions and we'll pull this off without a hitch. She'll be totally me and everything will be fine.

Astral Will flashed her maker another wide smile, then folded her list and put it into her jeans pocket.

"Sure, sure, I've got it," she declared.

"Thank goodness," Will sighed.

"I've only got one question," Astral Will interjected.

"Uh-huh?" Will responded skeptically.

"Hmmm," Astral Will wondered with wide eyes. "Who's this Will?"

"What?" Will cried. She sat her double down on the ground and crouched before her.

"We need to have a long talk," Will said to her double, sighing.

Twenty minutes later, Will emerged from the shell cave, just as Hay Lin was waving goodbye to Astral Hay Lin. The double gave Hay Lin a wink, then scampered over the boulders toward Heatherfield with a quick, light, and very familiar gait.

Will heaved an envious sigh. Adding insult to injury was the fact that Cornelia immediately began chatting with Hay Lin about their very successful astral drops.

"So, yours has hit the road, too, huh?" Cornelia said. "I said good-bye to my drop a few minutes ago. I think she'll do fine."

"Yeah!" Hay Lin marveled. "I've questioned her about all my habits, and it looks like she knows everything! She'll go home, lie down in my bed, and probably even have my dreams."

"While *we*, on the other hand," Cornelia scowled, "head straight into a nightmare!"

Will sighed. Cornelia was right. As their journey to Metamoor grew ever closer, her hands were feeling more trembly and her stomach was quaking.

It doesn't help, Will thought irritably, that my astral drop is–

"Ready," said a very familiar voice behind Will. "I think I'm ready!"

Will turned around to glower at Astral Will as she emerged from the shell cave. She was scanning Will's list attentively.

"Okay," Astral Will said. "At seven A.M. – wake up. Seven-fifteen – shower. At ten to eight, kiss Mum good morning. Then breakfast, then– "

"Okay, okay, I think you've got it," Will said sternly. "Listen, if you just follow the instructions, you can't go wrong. And remember– "

"I know, I know," Astral Will interrupted impatiently. She was slinging her leg over Will's red bike. "I'll study what I'm *not* supposed to do. You've written those things in bold and underlined each one three times!"

Before Will could say anything else, Astral Will gave her a cavalier wave and began to pedal away. Will watched her double go, then hung her head in worry.

"Oh, man," she sighed. "I hope she finds her way home, at least."

She felt Irma's sympathetic hand on her shoulder.

"She'll be fine," Irma assured her. "It's us I'm worried about. We'd better hurry. Its time to head to Metamoor!"

SIX

With her fellow Guardians, Hay Lin watched Astral Will pedal up the hill and away. Then she turned to walk with them back into the looming shell cave. She gazed up at the scallop-shaped mouth of the cave and was transported – just for an instant – back in time. She and Irma were suddenly little kids again, playing hide-and-seek.

Then she, Irma, and Elyon were in the shell cave, giggling and toasting marshmallows over a campfire.

Next, it was summertime. Hay Lin had been bodysurfing all afternoon, and she'd sought shelter again in the cave, laying her sunburned self down on its cool, dark, sandy floor.

The place had always been a haven.

Now it was a gateway to the unknown.

Hay Lin sighed. "I've come to this cave thousands of times," she told the others. "I would never have expected it to be the site of a portal!"

As the girls plunged deeper into the cavern, darkness surrounded them.

"Hay Lin and I brought equipment," Irma said, pulling a flashlight out of her bag and clicking it on.

Oh, yeah, Hay Lin thought, shaking her head slightly. Stop daydreaming. It's mission time. She pulled her own flashlight out and shone it into the cave. The bright beam of light skimmed over a chaos of painted scrawls and etchings – words, initials, hearts, pictures – all mementos of people's time in the cave.

"There's so much graffiti on the walls!" Will gasped. "I didn't notice it before."

"Yup," Irma mused. She paused before a couple of inked phrases. The first said I LOVE ANNE. S.R. The next read ANNE + BILLY. SORRY, S.R.

"It's cutthroat," Irma said with a giggle. "He goes out with her one summer. And the same summer, she's dating someone else. Cruel! Every carving is a love story. They're little bits of history!"

Cornelia scowled.

"No they're not, Irma," she scoffed. "They're acts of vandalism!"

Cornelia skimmed her tapered fingers over the cave wall and squinted at the graffiti angrily.

"Now that I have the power of the earth," she said, "I realise more and more that people don't respect it!"

She's got a point, Hay Lin thought, with a nod. But she didn't have time to voice her opinion. Suddenly, on a section of almost-bare wall up ahead, she saw something.

Something that made her blood run cold.

Hay Lin made herself run to the wall.

"Look here!" she cried to her friends. They hurried after her. Breathing hard, Hay Lin slapped a hand onto the wall, right next to a picture. Unlike the other scrawls, this image was composed of blue paint. It was a cluster of four swirly flames.

"Blue fire, four flames," Will said dully. "So? What's the big deal?"

"It's the same one that Irma doodled in class this morning," Hay Lin cried. "In her diary!"

Irma gazed at the blue flames. Her eyes

widened in disbelief. This was unbelievable.

"That's impossible," she croaked. "I haven't been here for a year – at least!"

She put a hand on her furrowed forehead.

"I was lost in thought when I drew that," Irma added.

Suddenly, Will let out a muffled moan, and her knees buckled. She felt woozy. She fell backwards and would have hit the hard, cave floor if Cornelia hadn't caught her.

"Will!" Irma screamed, jolting herself out of her reverie.

Hay Lin knelt down next to Will and held her breath. Will's head lolled for a moment. But only a few seconds later, her big, brown eyes fluttered open, and she managed to give her friends a weak smile.

"Everything's okay, you guys," she rasped. "It's just the usual dizzy spell."

"The dizzy spell you have whenever you're near a portal," Hay Lin pointed out.

Ever since the girls had discovered their extraordinary powers, Will had been having those spells. Her head would fall forward onto her chest, and her face would become paper-white. She'd groan, and a cold sweat would break out on her forehead. The closeness of Metamoor made her ill. The one good thing about the attacks was that they also let the Guardians know when they'd hit their mark.

"Maybe this means the portal is here," Hay Lin said, staring in awe at the blue flames scrawled on the stone wall.

Will lurched to her feet and stood next to the bit of graffiti. She beckoned to her fellow Guardians. The girls joined hands and formed a semicircle around the image of the flames. Will shook away the last of her dizziness and gave each girl a serious look. When Will's eyes met Hay Lin's, Hay Lin tried to smile. She tried to draw on the strength and determination she saw in Will's eyes. This was no time to back down. She had to be brave – for Taranee.

"Let's try to open the portal," Will said somberly. "Stay strong. I'm going to touch the drawing. . . ."

Looking around, Hay Lin observed each girl's reaction. Cornelia's face remained unreadable. Irma's eyes were open and curious. And Will looked terrified. Hay Lin could only imagine what *she* looked like. She watched, with wide, fearful eyes, as Will's fingertips stretched towards the blue flames, reaching out for the next chapter in the Guardians' overwhelming destiny.

Here we go again, Hay Lin thought. It was another moment of truth. Once more, we are going to step through a doorway that seems to go nowhere. We are going to risk our lives because we are the Guardians. And what's on the other side? Who knows? But something will be there – waiting.

SEVEN

As Will clasped Cornelia's hand and got ready to touch the four blue flames painted on the cave wall, she felt a wave of uncertainty surge through her chest. She didn't want to admit it, but she was scared.

She glanced around the circle at her friends. On their pale faces, she could see the same fear that she was feeling.

But she also saw Cornelia's set jaw.

And Irma's stubbornly pouty lips.

And Hay Lin's fiery eyes.

They were *all* scared. But they were also superdetermined!

We're together! Will reminded herself as her fingers intertwined with Cornelia's.

That gave her the strength finally to touch

her hand to the scroll-like picture on the cave wall. She pressed her palm against the rock and closed her eyes. Then she waited for the Heart of Candracar that was within her to work its magic. She expected to feel a bubble of energy well up inside her. Maybe a swirl of pink magic would envelop the quartet. Or perhaps the portal would burst open, flickering with blue flames. Maybe the tunnel would even ripple, just like the one that had opened in Mrs. Rudolph's attic.

Whatever happened, Will knew it would be dramatic.

She braced herself and waited.

And waited.

O-*kay* . . . she thought impatiently. Ready for some action!

But nothing happened. No pink swirls. No big, bad shafts of light. Nada.

Finally, Will opened one eye a crack and glanced around. Her hand was still placed over the blue drawing. She and her three friends were still standing, shivering slightly, in a cold, seaside cave. Each one of them had cautiously opened one of her eyes.

Finally, Will sighed in frustration and

dropped Cornelia's hand.

"Nothing happened!" she cried.

"Oh, sure it did," Cornelia cracked. "Magic kept us here among all this amazing artwork."

When Cornelia tossed out the careless barb, Will felt her shoulders sag.

First, I create a clueless astral drop, she thought. Then, I can't even open a portal.

Excuse me, Will thought, glancing at the ceiling – and towards the place where she imagined the Oracle of Candracar lived. Please remind me again *why* I'm the leader of this crew? Especially when I can't seem to do anything right?

Will must have been wearing her sadness on her sleeve, because suddenly Irma spoke up cheerfully.

"Don't worry, Will," she said. "I get faint sometimes, too. Usually, when it's been a long time since dinner."

Cornelia huffed and turned her back on Will.

"'Don't worry, *Will!' Pooooor* Will," she whined. "Shouldn't we be thinking about poor somebody *else* right now?"

Will felt as if someone had kicked her in the

stomach. Feeling short of breath, she whispered, "All you do is blame me for Taranee's situation, Cornelia. . . ."

As she rasped out the words, Will felt her hurt and her anger growing. Her voice grew shrill, and, before she knew it, she'd stomped over to Cornelia and leaned into her pretty, sullen face.

"You know very well that *she* was the one who asked me to leave her in Metamoor," Will cried. "She did it to save us."

Will's outburst seemed to crack Cornelia's icy veneer. She actually seemed startled and – perhaps – even a little remorseful? Her voice was less edgy as she replied, "I'm not saying that Taranee didn't speak to you. I'm only saying that I wish I'd heard her, too."

"No! You don't!" Will almost screamed. She felt her lip tremble and her eyes well up with tears. "You're lucky! You don't hear Taranee's desperate cry echoing around your head every hour. Every minute! Every . . . every *second*!"

Will flung her backpack to the ground and fell to her knees, burying her face in her hands. Her body was shaking with sobs now. Her guilt – and Taranee's grief – had been weighing upon her from the moment the girls had returned to Heatherfield. Now she had finally reached her breaking point.

Will sniffed loudly, and her chest heaved with sobs. She didn't know if she'd ever be able to stop crying! She really *was* a terrible leader!

But suddenly, something broke through Will's grief. It was the light, cool touch of a hand on her shoulder. It was Cornelia's! In a tender and comforting voice, Cornelia whispered, "Will, I'm sor– "

"Shhhhh!"

That was Irma. And her voice sounded urgent.

"Listen!" she hissed.

A feeling of fear made Will catch her breath. With one last hiccup, her sobs subsided. She blinked away the tears in her eyes and peered into the cave. Irma's head was cocked intently.

"What?" Hay Lin whispered. "I don't hear anything."

"That's my point," Irma squeaked. "Where's the noise of the waves? The roar of the ocean?"

Suddenly, Irma spun around.

"And that's not all," she exclaimed, pointing

at the ceiling. "Look, there's a weird, glowy light in here all of a sudden."

Irma turned off her flashlight to prove her point. Will gasped. Irma was right. The cave, which should have been pitch-black without the flashlight beam, was filled with a wavery, blue light.

"And the cave walls have become all smooth and glassy," Irma added. "Like the inside of a real shell!"

No sooner had Irma said the word "shell" than Will heard an echoey, distant roar. It sounded just like the inside of a shell when she cupped it around her ear to hear the ocean!

"What is that?" Will asked anxiously, glancing over her shoulder.

Then she screamed.

The ocean sound in a seashell was usually just an illusion. But what she saw was real – a giant gush of roiling water, crashing through the cave and heading straight for the Guardians. It was going to engulf them!

"Water!" Hay Lin screamed. "Lots and lots of water!"

Cornelia threw herself against Irma as the water began to swirl around the girls' feet.

"Irma!" she cried. "Do something!"

Acting seemingly on instinct, Irma thrust out her arms beside her. In a steely voice, she announced, "I'll create a bubble of air!"

Will felt the water rise around them. She sucked in a desperate gulp of air and held her breath. Then she squeezed her eyes shut and grabbed onto Cornelia and Hay Lin for some much-needed support.

She gasped as the cold water swirled around her legs. It quickly rose to her waist. Then her chest. Then her head!

"Aaaaaagh!" Will screamed.

She gasped and screamed again.

Before she could scream a third time, she realised something.

I just breathed! she thought incredulously. I gasped and didn't suck in a lungful of water.

Will's eyes flew open. Irma had done exactly what she'd said she would! She'd created a giant, bobbly air bubble around the four of them. Now, they were bouncing along peacefully in water that surrounded them on all sides.

Will heaved a sigh of relief and flashed Irma a triumphant thumbs-up. But she didn't have time to savour their survival. They had to figure out what to do next! And where they were headed.

Will spun around and pressed her hands to the balloonlike wall of the air bubble. She peered around, but all she could see was the walls of the cave. They were still smooth and glassy. The walls had also lengthened into a long tunnel – a tunnel that was transporting their air bubble at a rapid pace.

"That was no tidal wave," Will declared. "This is a portal. We're crossing over into Metamoor!"

Hay Lin pulled her backpack off her shoulders and began yanking heavy, shapeless cloaks out of it. They were made of nubby, brown fabric.

"Quick! Put these on," she ordered the girls, tossing each one a garment.

"What kind of fashion faux pas are these?!" Cornelia asked, regarding her cloak with a curled lip.

"Hey, don't dis the designer," Irma said, squirming into her own cloak. Its floppy hood completely covered her honey-coloured hair.

"Don't worry about it," Hay Lin said. "They

are pretty ugly. Like monks' robes. They're the same things I remember seeing the people in Meridian wear."

"Brilliant!" Will cried, pulling her own cloak around her shoulders. "This way, we can be less suspicious."

"That's what I was hoping," Hay Lin said. "Of course, we don't even know if we're in the right place."

"We'll find out soon enough," Cornelia pointed out, pressing her hands to the wall of the air bubble. "There's a light up ahead. We're heading out of this tunnel!"

Will clutched at Cornelia's robe. Hay Lin and Irma threw their arms around each other. As the bubble plunged through the mouth of the tunnel, they looked around. And then together, they all began to quake!

"If this is what's outside," Hay Lin cried, "I want to go back inside! Now!"

"We're . . . we're . . . specks!" Irma cried. "We're floating around in nothingness!"

Will nodded in agreement. A nod was all she could muster. There was no way she could talk. She was petrified. Where were they? She peeked over her shoulder at the giant cave from which the girls had emerged.

It *was* a seashell!

That's impossible, Will thought. There's no seashell on earth big enough to dwarf four girls like us.

Will turned back to her friends to see what they thought. Their faces told her that they were occupied with other worries – namely, the giant, glassy orb looming right in front of their air bubble!

In the center of the orb was an inky dot, as looming and menacing as a black hole.

Around the dot was a shimmery circle of green.

And around *that* was a sea of white, threaded with craggy, red seams.

A glassy, blue shade of some sort closed over the orb. Just as quickly, the shade lifted. Then it lowered and lifted again.

Almost like a blinking eyelid, Will thought.

A blinking . . . eyelid?!?

Suddenly, Hay Lin squealed and fell backwards, landing on the floor of the bubble with a plop. Cornelia hunched down over her knees in fear. And Will grabbed Irma's elbow, clutching her friend's arm with a strength born of terror.

They were trapped in a bubble with no way to escape. Nothing they had encountered before could have prepared Will for what she was now looking at. This was unbelievable – and terrifying.

"Irma?" she squeaked. "That nothingness you mentioned? Well, it's looking right at us!"

EIGHT

"*Aaaaaaaaagh!*" Will, Cornelia, and Hay Lin shrieked, clinging to each other in horror.

But Irma couldn't muster up the breath to scream. She was too busy. One part of her mind was focused on – duh! – being terrified. But another part of her, the part that was a magical Guardian, had to concentrate on keeping herself and her friends alive. Without Irma's air bubble, they were sunk – literally!

So, even as Irma gaped at the giant eyeball – which was scrutinizing the girls between slow, lazy blinks – she had to keep blue magic pulsing from her palms, breathing life into their air bubble, and keeping the water at bay.

Speaking of water, Irma thought, what kind of odd ocean are we floating around in anyway? Time to scope out the situation!

Luckily, the giant eyeball chose that very moment to rise up, up, up, and away from the Guardians. As Irma craned her neck to peer at the retreating orb, she gasped.

She was staring straight at a lumpish, blue, Metamoorian creature – another one of the ogres that had been terrorising the Guardians ever since they had first acquired their powers. And just like the other big, blue baddie in their lives, this dude was unspeakably ugly. His big, potatoey head was flanked by pointy, fuzzy ears and grey, rocklike lumps. His neck was nonexistent. His hands, which were clutching a tall glass of water, were awkward, pudgy, and tipped with dirty claws.

The only difference between this blue guy and the other blue guy? The first villain – Vathek, as Irma had heard him called the last time they had been in Metamoor – was only about twice the size of the girls. *This* ogre was at least *one hundred* times as big as they were.

He was peering down at the girls with a devilish grin. And that's when Irma noticed something else.

He was dry!

Whereas, we're all wet! Irma thought. We're inside some container of water in this giant's house. Now I know how Jack the Giant-Killer felt!

Suddenly, the blue creature opened his mouth to say something. Irma couldn't have been more shocked at his first utterance.

"Mummy!" he cried. The creature's voice was thick and phlegmy, but also high-pitched.

"He's just a kid!" Will hissed in Irma's ear.

"Come and see, Mummy!" the kid cried again. As he slammed his giant water glass down near the girls' container, Irma began to wrap her brain around this new reality. They were inside a glass bowl, on a wooden table, in a mammoth house. They were this giant, blue kid's new pets!

"I'm cooking dinner, Fargart," a deep, rumbly voice called from the distance somewhere. "I can't come and see."

The blue kid – Fargart – trotted away. So Irma and her friends had a chance to look around. The room looked like the interior of a medieval castle: looming Gothic furniture, tapestries, and Tudor-style windowpanes. The walls were made of stone blocks, and the light was dim.

Yup, Irma thought with a nod. We're in Metamoor, all right. The last time the girls had landed in that gloomy world, the architecture had all looked like this – cold, forbidding, and ancient.

Irma's ears pricked up as "little" Fargart ran into another room and began chattering excitedly to his mother.

"That hermit crab I found at the market is coming out of its house," he announced.

"That was only an empty shell," Fargart's mum said from the next room. Then Irma heard a squishing sound. She cringed.

I wonder what Mum's cooking for dinner, she thought with a shudder. Sautéed space aliens? Or maybe . . . eggs with a side of humans!

"You need to stop picking things up off the ground," Fargart's mum admonished him.

"I didn't pick it up," the boy protested. "I found it!"

"Girls, I've got a terrible feeling about this," Will said, turning to her friends. "Clearly, we're in Metamoor. But we're also really, *really* small!"

"*And*," Irma piped up, "We seem to be floating around in some kind of glass bowl."

"Uh-huh," Will said. She gazed up at the circular rim of the bowl, which loomed seemingly hundreds of feet above them. "The thing that worries me is, I know of only one reason a kid would have a glass bowl filled with water."

"Are you saying," Hay Lin asked, clutching at Irma frantically, "that somewhere in here we might see a little . . . fish?"

"A *big* fish!" Cornelia squealed, pointing to a stack of rocks near the girls' bubble.

"Aaaaaaaagh!" the Guardians shrieked in unison.

They were looking at another giant eye.

But this eye was black and soulless. And it was attached to some sort of green, aquatic creature with fins, a tail, *and* eight legs! The fish's puckering mouth was lined with jagged, yellow teeth, and its inky eyes looked decidedly . . . hungry!

Irma clutched at her friends and squeezed her eyes shut in horror.

Okay, she thought as she felt every bone in her body begin to tremble. I think I *finally* understand what my English teacher means when he talks about "irony." Irony has to do with the fact that one of my kindred spirits – a water-dwelling sea creature – is going to eat me up!

Irma covered her face with her hands, unleashed one anguished sob, and then waited for the giant fish's teeth to slash into the girls' air bubble. The fish would soon begin gobbling the girls up, one by one. She braced herself to feel horrible pain.

But instead, she felt power!

Irma was sensing the telltale presence of the girls' mystical strength. She peeked out through her fingers and saw swirls of silver, blue, green, and pink enveloping them all like a protective blanket. Then Irma felt a shaking. And a shuddering.

And a swooping. Now it was the Guardians who were going up, up, and away. They were hurtling toward the ceiling.

They were growing!

Irma felt a quick bite of pressure on her arms and legs. Then she heard the tinkling of breaking glass. The girls had burst out of their fishbowl. Finally, their feet hit a stone floor.

Irma glanced around the room. The table was now about waist-high. The chairs were short enough for the girls to sit in.

"We're back!" Irma cried, jumping up and down.

"Yeah, and we're about to get caught," Cornelia hissed, jerking her thumb towards the kitchen door. Two rumbly voices were drawing closer.

"I want *you* to see it, mummy," Fargart was urging his mother.

"Oh, all right," the girls heard her say.

"Quick," Hay Lin squeaked, pointing at the tall, Gothic windows. "Let's make a getaway to safety."

She closed her eyes and thrust her palms toward her friends. Silver swirls began to emanate from her hands. She was going to use her magic to fly the Guardians through the nearby windows.

As Irma watched Hay Lin work her magic, she silently corrected her friend. We'll see what kind of safety we can find in Metamoor, she thought with a shudder. Then she braced herself for the magical teleportation. But just before Hay Lin's power spirited the girls away, Irma's eyes fell upon something flopping around near her shoe. It was the multilegged green fish. It was writhing and gasping pathetically.

Irma felt a pang of pity.

Okay, so a few seconds ago this critter was looking at me like a side of fries, she thought with a shrug. But still, he is a water-dweller. I can't help thinking he's cute.

Irma held up her hand.

"One second," she told Hay Lin.

"What?!" Cornelia sputtered. "You'll get us caught!"

Irma ignored Cornelia's comment and bent over to scoop up the poor, flopping fish. She plunked him into the glass of water that was still standing among the shards of broken fish-bowl.

"All right!" Irma said, nodding at Hay Lin.

Whooooooosh!

For a moment, Irma couldn't breathe. A swirl of air around her seemed to pull all the oxygen from her lungs.

An instant later, she and her friends were standing on the other side of the tall, now-open window. They stumbled for a moment and clutched at each other for balance. That's when they heard the mother scolding her little boy again.

"Fargart!" she bellowed. "Your fishbowl is broken all over the floor! Is this any way to take care of your things?"

"What?" Fargart cried. "But where's my carnivorous spiderfish?"

Spiderfish? Irma thought. *Carnivorous?!*

"Here it is." Irma could hear the mother plodding heavily over to the table. She must have been looking into the water glass. "Poor fishie. Look at how it's trembling. It's terrified!"

"I . . . don't understand," Fargart squealed.

"Well, maybe your father will help you understand," his mother announced. "You and he can have a long talk when he gets home."

Irma couldn't help but giggle.

"I adore our powers," she said. "We keep discovering new things they can do. Like restoring us to our proper size."

"Just in time, I'd say," Cornelia said. She nudged her cloak's heavy, brown hood off her head so she could look around. The Guardians were standing on a crowded, cobblestoned street lined with grey, stone buildings. The air was hazy with soot and dirt. And it didn't smell so great, either.

Apprehensively, the girls tiptoed down the

empty street. Irma found herself pulling her cloak more tightly around her and shivering.

"Taranee must be here somewhere," Will said, as the girls rounded a corner.

"And so are a bunch of monsters," Irma said in a quivering voice. "Remember what it was like here before? Lizardy creatures and big, lumpy, blue guys and scaly, dreadlocky Mrs. Rudolph types?"

She looked to her friends. Will and Cornelia gave her trembly nods. But Hay Lin only smiled peacefully. As she walked – make that glided – down the bumpy street, the smallest Guardian closed her eyes and cocked her head, yet she never stumbled or tripped.

"Hay Lin?" Cornelia blurted. "What's with you?"

"Nothing," Hay Lin replied without opening her eyes. "The air of Metamoor's streets is talking to me! I smell its perfumes. I hear the sound of its voices. I think these monsters are not so different from us after all!"

Irma looked at Hay Lin's face. Her bud seemed so serene – happy, even! As the five girls walked into a courtyard milling with Metamoorians, Irma willed herself to follow her friend's example – to restrain herself from shuddering in disgust. And that was when she really saw what Hay Lin was talking about. Though this Metamoorian city's dwellers looked about as different from the Guardians as they possibly could, their activities were familiar. Green, scaly youths were chasing a ball around the cobblestoned street. A tall lizard in a brown cloak was buying some blue vegetables from a street cart. A couple of plump, flat-snouted creatures were giggling and clutching schoolbooks.

Those girls might be our age! Irma marveled. They are really just like us, dashing home for an after-school snack and gossiping about cute boys.

Suddenly, Irma was looking at the bustling city with a gleam in her eye. Hay Lin practically spoke her thoughts.

"The last time we were here," Hay Lin declared, "I felt like an outsider. But today, it frightens me less!"

Irma kept looking around. When her eye fell upon a little store tucked between a grisly butcher's shop and a parchment-filled newsstand, she grinned.

"I've got an idea," she said. "As long as we're feeling brave, why not start unraveling Metamoor's mysteries? How about right there!"

She pointed at a store filled with all sorts of mysterious wares. In the window, Irma saw parchment scrolls and telescopelike instruments. She saw orbs that looked like crystal balls and mortars and pestles just made for a witch's workshop. She saw . . . adventure.

"Um, I don't know," Will responded shakily. "We've got to fly below the radar here."

"Come on, Will! Look at that dusty old shop," Irma said. "Do you think *anyone* goes in there? I just want to take a quick peek around. Five minutes. You won't be sorry!"

Then she trotted across the street towards the shop.

Irma stuck to her promise, and, a few minutes later, the girls were walking through Metamoor's streets once again. They'd pulled their faces deep within their cloaks' shadowy hoods. Irma no longer felt chilled and shivery. Their browse through the bizarre shop had whipped her into an excited sweat.

Or maybe she was just feeling the heat of

Will's glare. Her stare was harsh!

"I'm so mad at you, Irma!" Will suddenly cried.

"Why?" Irma demanded in surprise.

"You shouldn't have talked to that shop-keeper," Will said. "Do you want Phobos and his followers to find out about us?"

"Please," Irma said, waggling the bell-shaped cuff of the sleeve of her heavy cloak. "In clothes like these, even Mrs. Knickerbocker wouldn't recognise us."

And our eagle-eyed school principal sees everything! Irma thought.

"Anyway," she continued out loud. "It was worth it. I traded him my watch for . . . this!"

With a dramatic flourish, Irma pulled her prize out from under her cloak and showed it to her friends. The blue ball cradled in her palm pulsed with glowing energy.

"Wow, a sphere," Cornelia said drily. "Do you kick it or eat it?"

"Wait a minute," Hay Lin said excitedly. She grabbed Irma's wrist and leaned over to take a closer look at the orb.

"Hey – that's a three-dimensional map of Metamoor!" she cried. "Wow! If you squint at it, you can even see people in miniature."

"Uh-huh," Irma bragged. "I've got the whole world in my hands, you could say. And look at this."

Irma turned the sphere around in her hands until she found a starfish-shaped building.

"See?" she said, pointing to the little star. "The shopkeeper told me that that's the castle of Phobos."

"Do you think Taranee is locked up inside there?" Hay Lin cried.

"I don't know," Will said, gently lifting the map from Irma's hand and peering at it with determination. "I guess it's possible. And if that *is* where she is, we've got a lot of ground to cover."

Will looked at Irma seriously. Irma saw fire in their leader's brown eyes.

"We *will* find Taranee," Will declared. "Even if we have to walk all over this entire planet!"

NINE

The Oracle floated – for the Oracle never needed to walk to transport himself – into the Circle of Knowing. This was his private observatory – a perfectly round, ornately decorated room deep within the Temple of Candracar.

Enormous as a country, but hidden away in the clouds of infinity, Candracar was, put quite simply, the place where good resided.

Its master was the Oracle, ancient but unbent and unlined. He saw all and knew all – all of the world's injustices and all its pain. Yet he still had faith that earth and its goodness would survive the war with Metamoor.

The Oracle had created the Veil that separated those worlds. He had also anointed the five young Guardians that now protected the

Veil. As he'd watched, they had begun to come into their own. They no longer feared their magic.

In fact, as the Oracle saw in his mind, they'd begun to use it in most creative ways. If only unwittingly, they'd even abused their powers. This by itself was not enough to furrow the Oracle's smooth forehead. But the brow of his adviser, Tibor, was another matter entirely. It had more than enough lines to make up for the ones the Oracle lacked.

As the Oracle projected his mind's images into different sectors of the Circle of Knowing, Tibor leaned over to view the scenes. In a brilliant shaft of green light, the petulant Guardian with the yellow hair was huddled at her desk over her homework.

The tiny girl, the one they called Hay Lin, was folding laundry for her mother in the silver beam of light.

The keeper of the Heart was getting into bed, a stuffed frog at her elbow.

All looked normal. But the Oracle knew that to be an illusion. Tibor, who'd been his adviser and his constant companion for centuries, sensed his lord's unease.

"Talk with me, Oracle," he said calmly, through his long, white beard.

"Good, Tibor," the Oracle said quietly, glancing up from the Guardians for a moment to give the old man a small smile. "You are aware of my gloomy thoughts. As you can see, the chosen ones have broken the laws of Candracar."

"I don't understand," Tibor said, scowling at the images. "They are simply living their lives."

"Those are not really the Guardians," the Oracle said. "What you see are magical creations. They call them astral drops."

Tibor shook his shaggy head in disbelief.

"They are perfect copies," he marveled. "The Guardians have become skillful with their magical powers."

"Don't praise them," the Oracle admonished. He floated a hand over the image of Will, making it large and three-dimensional. She was lying back in her bed, snuggling into her pillow. Her eyes closed, and a contented smile settled onto her face.

"It is their job to close the portals," the Oracle pointed out. "Not cross through them. And that is what they have done – twice now!"

"Must you punish them?" Tibor asked.

"I have to make up my mind," the Oracle said. He closed his eyes and clasped his hands together in front of him. Despite the immortality of his body, his shoulders felt heavy. The decision would require much meditation.

"They are traveling through the land of Prince Phobos," the Oracle declared somberly.

"They are risking everything!" Tibor cried. "For what?"

The Oracle opened his eyes. Sadly, he waved his hand over Will's image again. It shimmered away. In its place appeared that of a blue-eyed girl. Though she was human, she wore the long robes of Phobos, emblazoned with the green-and-white seal of Phobos – a circle edged in spikes.

Her name was Elyon.

If only that young girl knew the truth, the Oracle thought.

But truth had nothing to do with what Elyon was discussing right then.

"You ask me why they take such risks, Tibor," the Oracle said. He gestured at the fluttery image of Elyon. "*She* will tell you."

Lo and behold, Elyon spoke. "Friendship!"

she declared. She seemed to be answering Tibor's query. But in fact, she was addressing her prisoner and former friend – Taranee!

Taranee, still in her altered form – striped leggings, wild tendrils of hair, feathery wings, and all – was imprisoned in a bubble that floated in the center of an endless stone turret. The sunless chasm was chilly, so the young Guardian had conjured up a floating ball of fire to warm her hands.

Her back was defiantly turned to Elyon, who leered down at her from a niche carved into the turret wall.

"What does that word mean to you, Taranee?" Elyon challenged her prisoner.

"Definitely not the same thing that it means to you," Taranee spat. Though she answered, she refused to look at her captor.

"Those girls," Elyon said, her sly smile giving a slanted look to her pale blue eyes, "the ones you call friends. They've left you and created a perfect twin to take your place."

The Oracle felt Taranee's pain and doubt. He winced. Still, he continued to watch the scene play itself out.

Taranee glanced over her shoulder at Elyon

and snapped, "That's not true."

"Look at the well, why don't you?" Elyon said. She fluttered her hand over her head. Suddenly a body of water appeared, suspended fifty feet above Taranee's floating prison. The water rippled and glistened, then grew as silvery as a movie screen. A wavering image of Taranee – the astral Taranee – appeared in the well. She was smiling with contentment as her mother kissed her on the cheek.

The Oracle felt Taranee's shock.

That's an astral drop, Taranee thought (and thus, the Oracle did, too). An astral drop who's taken my place at home. Taken my cosy bed. Taken my mother! While I sit here, forgotten.

The Oracle felt Taranee's mind swerve to Will.

Will hasn't abandoned me, she thought. I told her to leave me here. What good would it have done if all of us had been captured? Of course, she and the others are working to rescue me! Elyon's just trying to divide us.

"I've had enough of your devious tricks," Taranee announced. This time, she spun around in her bubble to stare Elyon down.

Little Taranee, the Oracle thought, once so

timid, so cowed by her magic, has found a source of strength within her – a fiery power. That is fortunate. She'll need it.

"Why are you doing this to me?" Taranee demanded of Elyon. "Why?"

"I'm wondering the same thing," said a silky voice behind Elyon.

"Cedric," Elyon gasped, spinning around.

With Elyon's back turned and her attention diverted, Taranee collapsed weakly to the cold, glassy floor of her bubble. If Elyon hadn't detected the psychic cost of Taranee's defiance, the Oracle had. The minutes stretched slowly inside her prison. Taranee's hope – and her faith in her friends – was faltering. Even Guardians could be weakened, and Taranee was spiraling towards despair.

The Oracle sighed.

There was nothing he could do for this young girl. She would have to find salvation within herself.

When he was sure that Taranee's heart was beating steadily – if quickly – the Oracle left her. His omniscient vision swerved into Elyon's head. There he found a chaos of cruelty and confusion, devotion mixed with longing.

Cedric glared down his aristocratic nose at little Elyon. He towered over her in his imposing cloak with its daggerlike epaulets. But his face was narrow and sharp-edged. His blue eyes sparkled icily.

Elyon gazed up at the man with an expression of slightly wary adoration. Her smug smile disappeared.

As he led Elyon away from the chasm, out of earshot of Taranee, Cedric said, "Explain, if you will, Elyon."

"Taranee is the weakest of the Guardians," Elyon said in a slightly trembly voice. "She's always been afraid of using her powers."

"And so?"

"Don't you understand?" Elyon said, without meeting Cedric's cold eyes. "I know how to get her on my side. On *our* side."

Cedric flicked a hank of his long, blond hair over his shoulder.

"Do as you like," he allowed. "But be careful. Taranee and her cage, her bubble, exist in tandem. She is at one with her prison. She could control it. But she doesn't know that."

"I know," Elyon said, a touch defensively. "But look at her."

Elyon and Cedric peered back down the dark, stone corridor. They could just barely glimpse Taranee's bubble. Inside, the Guardian was sobbing softly. The flame that crackled over her head was dimmed by her anguish.

The Oracle winced once again, but forced his mind to focus on Cedric's final words to his charge. "See to it that Taranee remains weak," he ordered Elyon. "Remain cautious. And try not to make her angry!"

As Cedric swept away down the hall, Elyon stood where she was, kneading her hands in anxiety. Then the Oracle felt her square her shoulders and get ready to face Taranee once more.

Meanwhile, Taranee was girding her strength as well. In fact, the Oracle could feel her sending telepathic messages out into the cosmos.

Will! Taranee was thinking urgently. Can you hear me, Will? I know you're somewhere. You . . . you *must* be there!

In Candracar, the Oracle clapped his hands together as he watched the girls. He couldn't help but feel proud of Taranee. Her hope was fading, he knew. But still, she persisted. She tried to connect with her friend.

Until, of course, she was interrupted by Elyon, who now appeared near her once again. Taranee's bubble floated very close to Elyon's perch. Elyon stared at the girl, her arms dangling impassively at her sides.

They really are like day and night, the Oracle thought. Taranee is all bright colours and passion. Elyon is pale and stoic in her long, white robe. And now, when they speak to one another, Taranee's voice trembles with feeling, while Elyon's is chilly and controlled.

"Hello, Taranee," Elyon said. "Have I come back at a bad time?"

Taranee was jolted out of her meditation. Then she whirled to face her captor.

"Elyon!" she yelled. "Are you here to tell me more lies?"

"No," Elyon said casually. "I just wanted to show you something. Something rather thought-provoking. Either you believe it or you don't."

Elyon waved her hand and, again, a bubbling mass of water appeared in the turret. This time, it roiled beneath Taranee's bubble. The Guardian peered down into it as an image began to form.

"Will!" Taranee cried as the picture solidified. She gaped at her friend, her . . . sleeping friend.

"Look how worried your friend is about your disappearance," Elyon said sarcastically. "Look how she's crying . . . thinking of you. . . ."

In Candracar, the Oracle sighed wearily. He glanced at the sundial built into an ornate archway at the entrance. Several earth minutes – and five Metamoorian hours – had passed since Elyon had begun tormenting Taranee. And Elyon – hardier than what her birdlike bones and wispy, straw-coloured hair revealed – was still at it. She was showing Taranee Will's progress through her morning.

It looked like an ordinary morning. Will arose from a warm bed, pulled on a pretty, pink shirt, and greeted a boy carrying a furry pet at the front door. The Oracle knew how much Taranee craved such mundane activities.

As the Oracle mused on this, he noticed a sudden shift of mood inside the Metamoorian turret.

With the appearance of the boy, Elyon had fallen silent. The Oracle swooped into her thoughts.

What's Matt doing at Will's house?! she was wondering. Why does the lead singer of Cobalt Blue care about a little dormouse? And Will's a Sheffield newbie, to boot! *Sigh* . . . he's just as cute as he was the day I left Heatherfield . . . days . . . weeks ago? I don't even know anymore. . . .

Elyon shook her head, as if to clear it of fog.

With a breezy nonchalance, Will was planting a kiss on Matt's lips! Next, she slammed the door in his stunned face.

The exchange of affection piqued Taranee's interest, too. The Oracle swung to her mind. She was laughing inwardly.

I've got her, the Oracle heard Taranee think. I've got her! Then she turned to her captor.

"What's wrong, Elyon?" Taranee asked Elyon tauntingly. "Why did you stop talking?"

"Mind your own business," Elyon snapped, turning sideways so Taranee wouldn't see her pale cheeks and trembling lower lip. "You just do your own thinking! You'll have plenty of time to do it, in your little bubble!"

"Will kissed Matt!" Taranee crowed. "And you have always had a crush on him."

"Shut up!" Elyon screamed. "No more!"

She spun around and disappeared, stomping down the hallway in anger.

For a moment, the Oracle felt triumph surge through Taranee's mind. But an instant later, her joy faltered. Next, it died, like a flame suddenly deprived of oxygen.

"Wait a minute," she whispered to herself. Tears welled up behind her round spectacles. "Elyon's really angry. Which means, what I've just seen – Will sleeping peacefully, Will kissing her crush – it's true! Will *has* forgotten about me!"

Taranee's shoulders began shaking with silent sobs.

As the Guardian wept, the Oracle transported his mind to Elyon, who was now stomping down a stone staircase. Cedric had appeared next to her again. His handsome countenance had disappeared, and he had taken on his snake form to hide his identity from the Guardians. His green chin jutted over his broad chest. Behind a pulsing, red mask, his eyes were hardened like black pebbles. The snake-man gave the girl a mischievous look.

"So . . . Will has just snatched a kiss," Cedric said to Elyon. "The kiss you always dreamed about. Are you envious?"

Yes, yes, yes! the Oracle heard Elyon scream inside her head. My heart is breaking into a million little pieces.

But what she said, wanly and without much feeling, was, "N– no, not envious. I'm faithful to you, Cedric!"

"Good!" Cedric declared smugly. He knew Elyon was lying to him. He expected it. Cedric, the Oracle knew, trusted no one.

He doesn't need to, the Oracle thought with another anxious sigh. He has many, many sources of information. And clearly, one of them has filled him in on some important news.

"To reward you for your loyalty," Cedric declared to Elyon, "I'll let you know that she was not your real rival. The actual Will is here in Metamoor!"

TEN

Beep! Beep! Beeeeeeeep!

Astral Will's hand disentangled itself from the blanket and groped for the source of the extremely annoying sound.

Aarrgh, she thought. This Will's bedroom is not only very messy, it's noisy. I don't understand this incessant beeping! Let's consult my little paper. Now, where did I put it?

Groggily, Astral Will – who had begun to think of herself as A.W. – sat up in bed. She looked around the room. There were stuffed frogs everywhere! Sunlight streamed into the room through tall windows flanked by pink curtains.

"Where is that list?" she whispered.

A.W. felt the beep pounding at the back

of her head. So she turned around. She found herself staring at yet another frog. This one had a clock in its belly. Squeezing her fingers into a fist, she thunked the frog on its head.

The beeping stopped!

Sighing with relief, A.W. slumped back onto her pillow. Then she glanced at the nightstand next to her bed.

Oh, yeah, she thought. There's the list Will made me. I was going to look at it, wasn't I? Let's see. . . .

A.W. picked up the paper and scanned it for the words *horrible, annoying,* and *beeping.*

"Huh," she whispered. "Nothing here about beeping. I guess I'm supposed to keep snoozing, then. Cool!"

A.W. was just snuggling back under the covers when her eyes skimmed over the frog clock. Its small hand was on the seven, and its long hand was on the twelve.

Seven o'clock, A.W. thought dully, as she flopped her pillow over her head.

Wait a minute, she thought suddenly. Seven o'clock!

A.W. shot upright once again and gasped, "The list said that at seven o'clock, the real Will gets up and goes to the bathroom to brush her teeth."

A.W. slumped to the bedroom door, rolling up the sleeves of her baggy, blue pyjamas.

Wonder where the bathroom is, she thought as she walked into the hall. She padded down the corridor, passing a kitchen. Once again, A.W. got distracted. First, she spied a table set with fresh-smelling bread, a crusty croissant, and a jar of chocolate spread. Then she noticed a slender woman in a pink bathrobe, slumped against the refrigerator. The woman unleashed a tremendous sneeze, then began talking into a phone with no cord.

"Yes, Amanda," she said in a very stuffy-sounding voice. "I've got a bad cold, so I'm going to stay home today. Could you cancel all my appointments?"

A.W. stared at the pretty woman for a moment. She felt some stir of familiarity in her gut, but maybe that was just the toast smell, making her hungry.

"Uh-huh, yes," the lady continued. "Tell Spencer to check the printouts and . . ."

Suddenly, the woman's big, brown eyes fell upon A.W. She gaped at her.

"Will, why are you still in your pyjamas?" she demanded.

"Uh, are you my mother?" A.W. responded.

The woman rolled her eyes. Then she turned her attention back to the phone.

"No, Amanda, I wasn't saying that to you," she said. "That was my daughter, who clearly is still mad at me for going on a date with her history teacher. I know – teenagers. So moody."

Uh, A.W. thought with a twinge, better keep moving. At least I know that she's Will's mother. I'm supposed to call her Mum. Now what was I doing? Oh, yes . . . the bathroom.

After scrubbing at her teeth and running a comb through her red hair, A.W. went back to Will's bedroom.

Now what? she thought wearily. Time to look at my directions.

A.W. scanned the room. Where was that paper? She walked over to the bed and peeked under the pillow. Then she pulled back the blankets. Then she looked under the bed. Then she searched under the desk, inside the closet, and in the toes of her bedroom slippers!

"I've lost it!" A.W. whispered in horror. She collapsed onto the bed and put a trembling finger to her chin. This was not good.

Okay, she told herself. Just try to remember what it said. At seven, wake up. Quarter past seven, brush my teeth and wash up. At seven-thirty, get dressed. At ten to eight, kiss . . . kiss. . . . Who am I supposed to kiss?

As she racked her brain, A.W. pulled a silky camisole out of a drawer and slipped it over her head. Then she shimmied into a pink shirt she found hanging in the closet. She was just fiddling with the pesky buttons when another noise filled the loft.

Dingdong.

That chime was much less irritating than the beeping, but still, it seemed to annoy the lady in the kitchen.

"Will," the lady called out.

Not the lady, A.W. reminded herself. Mum.

"Yes, Mum!" A.W. answered.

"Please answer the door," Mum yelled.

"Yes, yes," A.W. said. She padded back out of her bedroom. As she struggled with the buttons on her shirt, she noticed her bare legs.

My legs sure are skinny, she thought. And *brrr*, they're cold. Maybe I should have put on some pants before answering the door. Oh, well.

Now, how *do* you get these buttons closed?

A.W. reached the front door and pulled it open. Standing in front of her was a boy who was holding a scampery little dormouse. The boy had shaggy, brown hair and big, brown eyes and just the right amount of scruff on his chin. He inexplicably brought a goofy smile to A.W's face. Her heart quickened and her stomach went sort of bubbly.

I think Will must like this boy, A.W. thought. Which means I do, too! Very cool!

"Uh . . ." the boy stammered, "Will?"

"More or less," A.W. declared. "What do you want?"

The boy's startled gaze traveled from A.W.'s bare shoulder to her bare knees and back to her bare shoulder. Then he said, "Uh, I know you wanted me to watch your dormouse. But he kept my parents up all night. So I had to bring him back to you, ASAP."

The boy glanced apologetically at his watch.

"I realise it's only ten to eight," he said, "and you're not quite read– "

"What time?" A.W. cried. Ten to eight! she thought. That was on the list! Right now, she was supposed to . . . oh, right!

"Thanks for the reminder," A.W. said. She took a step forward and put her hands on the boy's shoulders. She pulled him toward her and planted a firm kiss upon his lips.

A.W. was dimly aware of the fact that the boy's eyes were growing wide and googly. His arms fell to his sides, leaving the dormouse with nowhere to go but into A.W.'s arms. It leaped over to her, then scampered up to her shoulder.

"Thanks for the dormouse, too!" A.W. said, cooing to the little critter and grinning. Then she stepped back into the loft and shut the door in the flummoxed boy's face.

"Whoever you are," she added, as she walked back to Will's bedroom. "Now, what was next? . . . Oh, yes, pants!"

A.W. hurried to Will's closet and pulled out a pair of jeans. As she was stepping into them, Mum poked her head through the bedroom door.

"Yesterday, when I came home, you were Miss Sulky," she declared. "Well, today, I'm staying home. Are you happy?"

"Uh . . . no, Mum," A.W. ventured.

"What?" Mum said. "Is this the same Will

who's always complaining that I work too much?"

"Okay, so, yes, Mum," A.W. declared. "Is that better? Jeez!"

Before Mum could reply, the dormouse skittered across A.W.'s shoulders and jumped onto the bed.

"Wait!" A.W. cried, chasing the little thing as it scrambled under the blankets. A.W. burrowed into the bed after it. She found herself blinking at both the dormouse – and her list!

"Ah, here it is!" A.W. exclaimed. When she emerged from under the covers, her mother had left the room. A.W. sighed with relief and scanned Will's instructions.

"Oops," she whispered. "At ten to eight, I was supposed to kiss Mum, not that boy. And . . . uh-oh! Number one on the list of *Don't*s was *Don't kiss any boys!*"

A.W. stared blankly at the wall. She'd done something wrong. But she didn't know what to do about it! There was nothing on Will's list about remedying big, fat mistakes.

A.W. thought for a moment. Or rather, she got as close to thinking as her astral drop mind would allow. Then she snapped her fingers.

Wait a minute, she thought. Mum just said she's staying home. For me! And what else do mums do? They provide guidance. They tell you what to do. Perfect!

A.W. walked back down the hall, zipping her jeans as she went. She peeked into the kitchen, where the real Will's mother was pulling a thermometer from her mouth and examining it.

"Mum?" she queried. "Have you ever been kissed by mistake?"

"What a question," Mum said. "No. But if I had been, that kind of mistake would have been paid back with a slap!"

"Uh-huh," A.W. replied. She frowned for a moment in thought. Then she nodded and looked at her watch. Uh-oh! She was going to be late for class at the Sheffield Institute! She dashed to the front door and slipped her feet into some lug-soled leather shoes. Then she pulled her grey coat from its hook.

"Will," Mum said. "Can you slow down for a minute? I want to tell you something."

"Not now, Mum," A.W. replied. "I have to make sure I stay on schedule!"

"You have a schedule?" Mum asked with a

bemused smile. "Yet it takes a cannon shot to get you up in the morning."

"Ah, that *beep-beep-beep*," A.W. said with a nod. "So that was a cannon shot! I'll have to make a note of that."

Mum got a funny look on her face. Then she noticed that A.W. was struggling with the zipper on her jacket. She zipped it up. She zipped it down. She zipped it up. She zipped it down. But the darned thing just stayed open!

"Let me do that," Mum said, walking over to A.W. She hooked the end of the jacket's zipper into a little slot. This time, the jacket zipped up and stayed closed.

"Cool," A.W. breathed.

"So, when you get home tonight," Mum said, "there'll be a dinner guest here."

"Uh-huh," A.W. said absently. Her eyes had just fallen upon the fragrant spread on the table. "Hey, is that croissant for me?"

A.W. dashed over to the table and took a quick bite of the flaky, crescent roll. *Yummmmm* –

"The thing is . . ." Mum said, with a mixture of nervousness, apology, and defiance. "Our guest is going to be Mr. Collins."

A.W. looked at Mum quizzically.

"So?" she asked, a few crumbs spraying from her mouth as she did.

"Maybe you're not understanding me," Mum said carefully. She gave A.W. a hard look. "We're talking about *the* Mr. Collins. Your history teacher."

"Good!" A.W. said. As she stuffed the last morsel of croissant into her mouth, she nodded with satisfaction. Maybe she'd get this Mr. Collins to help her with Will's history homework, which was probably hard and boring. Will would be pleasantly surprised when she returned!

"Have fun!" A.W. added, giving Will's mum a thumbs-up.

"Have . . . fun?" Mum sputtered back. She gave A.W. another strange look.

I wonder what that means, A.W. thought. Perhaps I've done the wrong thing again?

But before she had a chance to ponder that idea, or check Will's list one more time, she glanced down at her watch.

Oooh, only ten minutes to ride Will's red bike to school, she thought. Must dash!

With that, A.W. put a big smile on her face

and grabbed the bike out of the foyer of the loft. She flung open the front door and plunged further into Will Vandom's day. After the morning's adventures, she was sure everything else would be a piece of cake. She still didn't know why Will had been so uptight. But, she wondered as she pedaled to school, *I do hope I'm going in the right direction.*

ELEVEN

Cornelia and her fellow Guardians were tromping up yet another cobblestoned Metamoorian street, skulking in the shadows of yet more gloomy, imposing houses.

I wonder how long we've been here, Cornelia thought with a sigh. If only we could use our powers to find the castle we saw on Irma's map. Hay Lin could fly us there on a pillow of air. Or Irma could create a river that would float us there. Or I could coax the trees to pass us from branch to branch until we reached the castle, well rested and fresh as daisies.

The image of tree branches bouncing the girls across the land of Metamoor was so comical Cornelia almost laughed out loud.

There was just one catch. She was way too tired and cranky to laugh.

"Irma," she finally said impatiently. "Lemme see that map of Metamoor again. I want to know if we're even remotely closer to Phobos's castle. We've been searching for hours."

"All right, all right," Irma said. She began to rummage around inside her brown cloak. But she froze when a voice rang out in the street.

"There she is!"

Irma gasped and looked up.

"There *he* is," she cried.

Cornelia and her friends followed Irma's gaze. And what they discovered was *not* good.

A big, brooding, blue-skinned brute with red, greasy hair and a serious underbite was pointing at Irma.

And the guy's not alone, Cornelia thought desperately. He's got about *twenty-five* green-skinned soldiers with him!

"Yikes!" Irma squealed. She turned on her heel and started running down the street.

"C'mon!" she screamed over her shoulder to her friends.

They began pounding after her.

And then, the hulking, scaly army began pounding after them!

"Okay, Irma!" Will demanded between huffs and puffs. "Who's that guy? And more importantly, who's his army?"

"He's the vendor who sold me the map," Irma cried.

Hay Lin was running next to Irma.

"Obviously, he wasn't satisfied with your watch!" she said, scowling suspiciously.

"I don't know why not!" Irma declared. "It's perfectly decent. I found it in the bottom of a cereal box."

"Ugh!" Cornelia said in disgust. Then she saw a staircase that veered off the narrow street.

"Up there!" she screamed.

Will was the first to veer off and begin racing up the stairs. Even though the girls were running for their lives, Cornelia couldn't help but smile a tight, satisfied smile. For once, Will had followed her lead. So, why not try again?

"Will," she gasped as they hurried up the stairs. "Don't you think it's time to transform ourselves?"

"No," Will said, with a quick shake of her

head. "The right moment hasn't come yet."

"What?!" Cornelia yelled. "Listen. You may hold the Heart of Candracar, but you're talking about *our* lives here!"

"I didn't ask for this responsibility," Will declared, shooting Cornelia a surly glance. "But since I *am* the keeper of the Heart, there's nothing you can do but follow me."

Cornelia was about to hurl a nasty retort at Will. But before she had the chance, the Guardians reached the top of the stairs.

They stopped cold.

They had arrived at the top of a landing – surrounded on three sides by looming, windowless walls. It was a dead end!

A dead end that *I* led us to, Cornelia thought with a gasp. Um, maybe Will has a point. For once, Cornelia felt grateful that the other girls were looking to Will for guidance. Because, frankly, Cornelia had *no* idea how they were going to get out of this fix.

Espccially with an army gaining on them every second.

"I hear them coming!" Irma squeaked, peeking over her shoulder at the staircase. Cornelia, too, could hear the rumble of angry voices and the thunder of dozens of feet. (Were they hooves? Claws?! Cornelia wondered desperately.)

Will stared in complete shock at the unclimbably smooth walls towering above them.

"A staircase that ends in a blank wall?" she breathed. "How is that possible?"

A raspy voice suddenly echoed out of nowhere.

"Everything is possible, here in Metamoor," the voice declared.

Cornelia looked wildly around the alley.

"Wha – aahhh!" she screeched.

The voice had come from a *hand* – a fleshy hand clad in what looked like brown armadillo skin. The hand was not attached to an arm or any other body part. It jutted out of one of the stone tiles of the landing's floor, like a wild weed that had taken root in a cement sidewalk.

The hand's plump forefinger waggled, beckoning the girls towards it. Then it pointed downwards at a square of darkness on the floor. The whole landing was cloaked in shadow, but this particular part was pitch-black.

"You have no alternative," the creepy voice

declared. "Enter the shadow now!"

Will cast a wild, fearful look at her fellow Guardians. Then she glanced over her shoulder. Cornelia followed her gaze. The leader of the pack of soldiers was only about twenty steps behind them.

"I saw them," he growled to the soldiers behind him. "They're up there!"

"The hand is right," Will said, shaking her head in disbelief even to be uttering such a ridiculous phrase. "We have no other choice."

Without another word, Will ran three steps and jumped onto the black square.

Make that *into* the black square. Will plunged through the floor as if it were made of paper. Suddenly, she was gone!

The remaining Guardians gave each other quick glances. Then Irma started running. Hay Lin was on her heels. And Cornelia was right behind her!

Hop! Skip! Jump!

Cornelia was the last to plunge into the shadow. She felt herself falling swiftly. But it wasn't a hurl-inducing free fall. Instead, Cornelia felt something buoying her up, like a virtual parachute, or some sort of safety net.

Whatever the force was, it allowed Cornelia to land on another cold, stone floor as delicately as a bird. In the pitch-dark, Cornelia blindly felt around for her friends.

"Are we all here?" Will asked.

"Here!" Hay Lin piped.

"Me, too," Irma said.

"And me," Cornelia answered. "Now, the real question is, are those guys going to be joining us, too?"

Together, the Guardians held their breath and braced themselves for the roar of soldiers tumbling after them. But a few moments of silence convinced Cornelia, at least, that they were safe.

Relatively safe, anyway.

"I can't believe this," Irma said.

Suddenly, the rumbly voice – the voice of the hand that had spoken to the girls up on the landing – pierced the darkness.

"Forget the laws of physics that regulate your world, Irma," it said.

"How do you know my name?" Irma cried into the blackness.

"Wait a minute," Will said. "That voice . . ."

A dull, white light erupted in the center of

the shadow. The light emanated from a small, glowing pyramid. And that pyramid rested on the hand of–

"Mrs. Rudolph!" the four Guardians cried. They blinked in shock at their maths-teacher-turned-monster. She was still in her Meta-moorian shape. Jutting out of her long, red dreadlocks were wide, floppy ears. Her face had a mass of crusty jowls and in its center, a squashy snout. Dotting her fleshy neck were three red horns. Her eyes were blood-red. But they were also, strangely, kind.

As were Mrs. Rudolph's words.

"I don't want to harm you, even if I should be angry with you," she announced, holding her source of light out toward the girls. "You forced me to abandon my home on earth. But . . . well, you're still my former students, and I still care."

With gratitude in her voice, Will said, "You move well in the dark. Is this where you live now?"

"This is not the dark," Mrs. Rudolph retorted. She let the pyramid go free, and it floated from her hand. It drifted out in front of her and began bobbing away. Mrs. Rudolph followed its light and the Guardians, followed her in silence.

"This is only Metamoor's immense underworld," the teacher explained.

Cornelia gazed above her. Mrs. Rudolph was right. They were surrounded by tall pillars and hardy crossbeams – an entire infrastructure that must have been supporting the city up above.

"You're hiding down here," Will said to their teacher quietly. "Just like you hid in our world. But from what?"

Over the dull glow of the pyramid, Mrs. Rudolph addressed the girls, with weariness in her red eyes and in her voice.

"There's a cloud that covers our sky and the hearts of our people," she said sorrowfully. "We are millions of black hearts. Anger. Desperation. This is Metamoor. This is the true darkness."

Cornelia hung her head. Mrs. Rudolph's despair was infectious. But then a thundering boom made her, and everyone else in their crew, jump! And then it came again!

Ftoooom!

Okay, Cornelia thought drily. So much for our soulful moment. Can't a Guardian get a moment of silence ever?

FTOOOOOM!

The noise was stronger now. Its thunder echoed through the cavernous space.

"Those *boom*s are not a good thing," Mrs. Rudolph said gravely. "What shall we do? You must decide quickly. Even in Metamoor, time does catch up with you."

"What do you mean by that?" Will asked her. "Is time different in Metamoor?"

"Why, yes," Mrs. Rudolph said. "In this prisonlike world, time passes much more slowly than it does on earth."

"What?" Will squeaked. "So, one earth day equals how much Metamoor time?"

"One or perhaps two weeks," Mrs. Rudolph said, shrugging her plump shoulders.

"Taranee!" Will wailed, clapping her hand to her forehead. "I've left her in the hands of those monsters for all that time?"

Once again, Cornelia didn't envy Will her position of leadership. She even sympathised with her. Her belief that Will was to blame for Taranee's predicament was definitely receding as their own present situation veered further and further out of their control.

Down here, Cornelia thought desperately, "control" is a fantasy. Who knows what to expect next?

FTOOOOOMMM!

Well, maybe I *do* know what to expect next, Cornelia thought, as the *boom* rang in her ears. Another confrontation. Another flight from death!

Meanwhile, Mrs. Rudolph had laid a crusty hand on Will's shoulder.

"Don't blame yourself," she was saying to her. "You couldn't know."

Suddenly, Hay Lin stepped toward the teacher.

"My question is, how do *you* know?" she demanded coldly. "How do you know why we're here? Who are you, really?"

Cornelia blinked in surprise at Hay Lin's display of suspicion.

Of course, I guess I would be doubtful, too, Cornelia thought, if the last time I'd seen Mrs. Rudolph, she'd tied *me* up and thrown me in the closet.

Because that's exactly what Mrs. Rudolph had done when she'd caught Hay Lin and Irma sneaking around her house. It had been a desperate effort on Mrs. Rudolph's part to avoid being discovered as an earth intruder. But the effort had failed when Will had discovered her friends and rescued them with the Heart of Candracar's magic. That was the reason Mrs. Rudolph had fled to Metamoor.

But now, the teacher was not going to be cowed. After all, this was her turf. So, she merely gave Hay Lin an impassive gaze and announced, "Today's lesson has come to an end, girls. The bell is ringing."

Mrs. Rudolph began to shimmer away! In an instant, she'd evaporated, like a puff of steam. And the moment she was gone, another *ftoooom* rang through the underworld. The girls dodged a sudden shower of rocks, which was followed by a shaft of light.

FTOOOOOOMMMM!

Terrified, Cornelia clung to her friends and peered upwards. A large hole was breaking through the ceiling. Peering down through that opening were the venomous snake-creature and his blue sidekick, Vathek!

Cornelia cringed and got ready to scream. But then she realised something.

When Mrs. Rudolph had disappeared, she'd

taken her glowing pyramid with her. Once again, the Guardians were cloaked in darkness. As long as they stayed away from the shafts of sunlight shining down into their hiding place, they were as good as invisible!

That is, *if* everyone stayed quiet.

"Ah– " Irma began to scream. Cornelia reached over and clapped her hand over Irma's mouth. "Shhhh," she whispered to all the girls. "Let's hear what the bad guys have to say."

They didn't have to wait long. Vathek let forth a guttural laugh and announced, "Ha! I've opened a crevice."

"Wonderful work, Vathek," the snake-man replied calmly. Cornelia watched his face contort itself into a ghastly grin as he peered down into the darkness. "Now, all we have to do is find them!"

TWELVE

Deep within the shadows of Metamoor's under-world, Will clutched at her friends in terror. The snake-man and Vathek were lurking above them, threatening to drop down upon them at any minute.

Once again, we're in hiding, Will thought.

And once again, we're fleeing.

Will hung her head and heaved a shuddery sigh.

When will this end? she wondered desper-ately. When we're sitting in a cell next to Taranee?

Suddenly, she gasped.

Hey . . . she thought.

She turned to her friends and whispered to them excitedly: "I have an idea. It seems like a crazy one, but you'll have to trust me. Are you with me?"

"Of course," Hay Lin squeaked into the darkness.

"You got it," Irma said.

From Cornelia, there was a skeptical silence. Will held her breath. If Cornelia refused, her plan couldn't possibly work. She braced herself for one of Cornelia's trademark barbs, or a shrill argument. But what she got instead was so surprising it moved her almost to tears.

Cornelia reached out through the blackness and found Will's hand – her right hand, the one that housed the Heart of Candracar. She squeezed it. And then, the most reluctant Guardian uttered one simple word.

"Yes."

"All right!" Will whispered. "Follow me."

The girls began creeping up a long stairway that seemed to be leading directly to the ugly gash Vathek had made in the ceiling. Will swallowed hard as the Guardians got closer to the light. With every step, her fear intensified.

But when she saw the giant, long-chinned serpent at the top of the stairs, her fear melted away. It was replaced by a wave of pure and absolute anger.

"So," the snake-creature was saying to his craggy, blue henchman. "We'll go down there and search."

The lump in Will's throat dissolved. In fact, with her friends behind her, she felt as though she could let forth a shout that all of Metamoor would hear. But she didn't have to. The beast's slithery tail was only inches from her face. So, Will merely announced, "Don't bother! We're right here."

The serpentine creature turned to gape at her. His eyes narrowed behind his red mask.

"You!" he growled.

"We have nothing to say to each other," Will said. She heard the other girls catch their breath behind her. She knew they were wondering *how* this could be a good idea. But she pressed on: "If you care to do anything to us, do it now!"

"Don't mind if I do," the creature said with a casual cackle. He waved his scaly hand at the girls. Will gasped as she felt her feet fly out from under her. Then she caught herself, just before her face banged into a pane of glass that had suddenly popped up before her.

In fact, the glass had formed a sphere all around her. She was floating in a bubble! But this one wasn't soft and pliant like the air bubble Irma had created for them. It was cold and smooth and flawless. It was also, Will realised as she pounded on the hard surface with her fists, impenetrable.

There was another difference, too. While the four Guardians had shared Irma's air bubble, now each one hovered – eyes wide with terror – in a spherical cage of her own.

"Here are your prisons, Guardians," he said to the girls with a menacing cackle.

In response, Will just glared at the monster. In the bubble cage next to hers, she saw frantic tears welling up in Hay Lin's eyes. Irma was speechless. She simply clutched her knees within her bubble and shivered.

The villain laughed at their fear. But the grotesque Vathek, peering into their glass cages with his beady little eyes, seemed utterly bewildered.

"I don't understand," he said to his master. "Why did they allow themselves to be captured so easily?"

"This world is immense," his master replied dismissively. "They have chosen the fastest route to a reunion with Taranee."

Will gasped. How could this beast have known? And now, her friends knew her plan also. She snuck shy glances at them.

Hay Lin's tears had dried. She flashed Will a defiant smile! Irma gave Will a thumbs-up. Even Cornelia arched her eyebrows in surprise. She was impressed! Will couldn't help smiling for a split second.

Of course, the feel-good moment lasted only for a second. Then the creature stepped in, as usual, with a buzz kill.

"I will grant you your wish," he said, swooping his snaky head down to make eye contact with Will. "And *you*, Will, shall give me the Heart of Candracar!"

Never, Will thought. But again, she refused to speak. Ignoring her silence, the towering villain rose up on his curly tail and announced: "First, though, there is someone who wants to see you personally."

He waved a meaty green arm, and suddenly Will was knocked off balance again! Her bubble, along with those of her friends, began skidding forward on a swath of whiteness. It was . . . snow!

We're on a sleigh ride, now? Will thought indignantly.

"What's happening?" she asked, as the girls sped through the snow. The snake-creature zipped along next to them, moving dozens of yards forward with every flick of his powerful tail. "Where are you taking us?"

"Nowhere," the monster spat. "The place you are about to see is denied to you. This is only a projection of . . . Phobos's garden."

As the words left the creature's mouth, the girls' bubbles swooped up off the ground. The blinding whiteness of the snow disappeared and was replaced with visions of such colour, and such scope, that Will could only blink at them in disbelief!

The Guardians' bubbles bobbled by a tree with a hundred sinuous trunks. Burnt-orange ferns waved and bowed. The Guardians saw mushrooms of the deepest burgundy; flowers that looked like ruffled lions' manes; sunflowers with petals of scarlet; eggplant-coloured rocks.

"It's . . . it's . . ." Irma stammered.

"It's useless to try to define it," the snake-man said with a leer. "Everything here is inspired by pure perfection."

"If it's so perfect," Will retorted, "then why do I have the creeps?"

It was true. Though her bubble was no longer skimming through snow, Will was still cold. Sadness dappled the flowers as surely as did sunlight. And, somehow, Will could feel that melancholy herself.

"Maybe you're scared because everything you see is *lethal*," the snake-man sneered. "Now, be quiet. Here they are. The Murmurers!"

The what? Will thought.

"These are the members of Phobos's court," the monster continued. "They are the voices and eyes of the prince of princes!"

The snake-creature clamped his thin-lipped mouth shut. For a moment, the garden was silent. But then, Will heard a low humming. No, not a humming. A hissing. A . . . whisper!

"*You . . . Guardians . . .*" hundreds of otherwordly voices said. "*You Guardians . . . earth . . . Guardians . . . earth . . .*"

Will gasped. Figures were beginning to

unfurl from the flowers! An elfin, golden creature with long fingers and hair like Spanish moss emerged from beneath a yellow stone. A sinuous blue female stepped from a bell-like bloom. Everywhere, the Murmurers were crawling into the open. This one with gleaming purple skin, that one with a long, turquoise mane, and still another with a body that was the bark of a tree.

"Their voices are barely whispers," Hay Lin exclaimed, as the creatures continued to murmur. "They're almost thoughts."

"What you see dims your other senses," the villain said. "Close your eyes and listen."

Though she was loath to do the snake-creature's bidding, Will was too curious to refuse the order. She squeezed her eyes shut. The murmurs swirled into her head.

"*You, earth Guardians . . . not worthy to approach us . . . may your end be quick. . . . May the Oracle learn to respect us. . . .*"

As the whispers drifted away, Will's eyes opened. She watched the Murmurers retreat back into their foliage.

"I don't understand," she cried.

"It's not important that you understand,"

the beast said. "What *is* important is that they have seen you. And now, you will see something else – the prison of Metamoor!"

Will cringed as their bubbles went for yet another swooping ride. But she barely had a chance to find her balance in her spherical cage before it came to a halt again. The four Guardians found themselves floating in a line in a tall turret constructed of stone bricks. The seemingly endless walls were interrupted at points by tall, arched niches.

"What a dreary place," Irma declared, gazing sullenly through her glass walls. "I bet those beauties in the garden don't know anything about it."

"They do not exist to live in Phobos's castle," the evil reptile-man said. He was looming before the girls, glaring down at them from a great height. "They live beyond its walls."

"And you?" Will said tauntingly. "Where is your place?"

"Here, for now," the snake-faced man responded. "Until, that is, you hand over the Heart of Candracar. Save yourself from the suffering you'll endure if you refuse!"

"Forget it!" Will answered, turning her back.

A moment later, she heard a reply. But it didn't come from the snake-creature. The voice was thin, girlish, and full of sarcasm.

"Wrong answer, Will!"

Will gasped.

Elyon! she thought. She spun around and stared at her former friend, who was walking into the turret from a long, dark hallway. Both her white cloak and her icy eyes made Will shiver.

But the thing hovering near Elyon made Will positively jump. It was another prison bubble. And floating within it was a girl with shiny black tendrils of hair and big, round glasses. She wore purple-and-turquoise leggings. And on her back, which was turned to Will, were a pair of sagging, despondent wings.

"Taranee!" Will screamed.

"Yes!" Elyon declared.

Out of the corner of her eye, Will saw the beast slither over to Elyon and hiss at her angrily. But Elyon just grinned and pointed smugly at Will.

Will didn't stop to wonder what the villains were whispering about. She had eyes for only one person.

"Taranee!" she cried to her friend's rounded back. "Talk to us. How are you?"

Cornelia reached out to Taranee anxiously. "Don't you want to see us?" she asked.

Taranee clapped her hands over her ears. Then, at last, she twisted around in her bubble to face her fellow Guardians. But instead of relief or gratitude, Will was shocked to see an unexpected emotion on Taranee's face – absolute rage!

"Quiet!" Taranee screamed at Will. "I don't want to listen to you! I don't ever want to see you again!"

THIRTEEN

Taranee gazed at the four girls, floating before her in bubble cages just like hers.

But they're *not* just like me, she thought angrily. I was loyal to them. I let myself be captured for them.

And what did they do? They went off and forgot about me. They left me to suffer in this tower with Elyon.

Taranee stared at her jailer. Elyon's pale eyes were slanting upward in a mischievous smile. She was relishing Taranee's pain. And that was when Taranee realised what Elyon was doing. She had conjured up those apparitions of Taranee's friends – so close yet so far away – to torture her. Well, Taranee wasn't falling for it anymore.

"You're not real!" she screamed at her fellow Guardians. She hoped her voice sounded strong, despite the great fear and disappointment she felt. "You're just images – artificial images! And I'm tired of seeing you. Go away! Just go away!"

"But, Taranee," Will gasped. "We– "

"Stop your tricks!" Taranee begged Elyon, clamping her hands over her ears again and squeezing her eyes shut. "I'll do anything you want, as long as you take me far away from here, right now!"

Taranee peeked through her fingers at Elyon to see if, for once, her mean, former friend would be merciful. But Elyon was paying no attention to Taranee. Instead, she had stomped over to Will's bubble.

"Do you hear that?" she asked Will tauntingly. "When I have finished with you, you will give us what we want – the Heart of Candracar!" The young girl's face was full of hate *and* satisfaction.

"You'll pay for this, Elyon!" Will spat back, pounding her hands on the bubble's glasslike walls.

"And *you* will grow old in this prison," Elyon

told Will. "You will never kiss your precious Matt again."

"If that's what you're worried about," Will said, "you can rest easy. The guy barely knows I'm a girl!"

Taranee blinked. Through the haze of her anger and anguish, she thought she'd heard Will say – Wait a minute!

"But I saw you!" Taranee declared, pointing at Will.

Now it was Will's turn to look confused. She and Elyon both stared at Taranee with mouths agape.

"Matt!" Taranee continued. "I saw you kiss him!"

"What?" Will cried, blushing deeply. "No! I've never kissed Matt!"

Suddenly, the snake-man slithered forward.

"Elyon," he growled. "Take Taranee away!"

Elyon scurried over to Taranee's floating bubble and began moving it toward the turret door. But before they reached it, they were stopped by Will's screech: "Wait!"

Will gazed at Taranee. And now, finally, Taranee allowed herself to meet Will's gaze. In her friend's eyes, Taranee saw confusion. And desperation. And . . . affection?

"Elyon played a trick on you!" Will cried. "You saw my twin – my astral drop – on earth! It didn't really happen!"

Taranee bit her lip. Could she believe Will? Or was it Will's astral drop who was saying those things? Elyon had Taranee's head spinning so fast she couldn't even begin to sort out who was who, or what was what!

Will – if that really was Will, Taranee thought – made one more attempt to reach her.

"If you don't believe me," Will said, "read my mind."

Elyon huffed impatiently. "Taranee– "

"Stop," Taranee growled, holding up one hand. She said the word with such power that Elyon *did* stop.

"Will is telling the truth!" Taranee said. "Only the real Will knows I'm telepathic!"

As she said the words, Taranee gazed into Will's brown eyes, which were beginning to fill up with grateful tears. The two Guardians – and best friends – faced each other in silence for a moment. Almost imperceptibly, Will nodded.

And in that one small but heartfelt gesture, she spoke to Taranee. Silently, she praised

Taranee for her strength. And she assured her that her ordeal – this particular trial, anyway – would be over soon. And she told Taranee that she had faith in her.

Will's friendship suffused Taranee with the first warmth she'd felt since entering her cell.

Looking around, Taranee felt her strength return. Her friends, her fellow Guardians, had come all this way to save her. Knowing that they had risked their lives, willingly facing danger, for her made Taranee's whole being warm with happiness.

A moment later, that warmth deepened – to fire. To wrath! Taranee turned inside her bubble to face her jailer, her tormenter – the cruel, cold Elyon.

"You have played with my feelings, Elyon," Taranee said. She pressed at the walls of her bubble with her magical hands. As she did, she felt the glassy substance begin to change! It warmed under her touch. It grew more pliant, more permeable. The magic was having an effect.

"But nobody," Taranee continued threateningly, "should be allowed to play with *fire!*"

Whooooosh!

Bursts of bright orange magic shot out from Taranee's palms. She arched her back and kicked out with her legs. And then she *broke* through the walls of her bubble! She was free! She soared through the air in a whirl of fire, preparing herself to face Elyon and the other enemies of the Guardians.

My captors, Taranee thought with rabid glee, are in for the fight of their lives! With my friends at my side, there's nothing I can't do!